# ACROSS THE
# FLOOR

Natasha Deen

ORCA BOOK PUBLISHERS

**Library and Archives Canada Cataloguing in Publication**

Deen, Natasha, author
Across the floor / Natasha Deen.
(Orca limelights)

Issued in print and electronic formats.
ISBN 978-1-4598-0920-8 (paperback).—ISBN 978-1-4598-0921-5 (pdf).—
ISBN 978-1-4598-0922-2 (epub)

I. Title.  II. Series: Orca limelights
PS8607.E444A77 2016          jc813'.6          c2016-900450-3
                              c2016-900451-1

First published in the United States, 2016
Library of Congress Control Number: 2016931894

**Summary:** In this high-interest novel for teen readers, football player Luc is
forced to take a dance class, where he discovers an unexpected new passion.

*Orca Book Publishers is dedicated to preserving the environment and has printed
this book on Forest Stewardship Council® certified paper.*

Orca Book Publishers gratefully acknowledges the support for
its publishing programs provided by the following agencies:
the Government of Canada through the Canada Book Fund and the Canada
Council for the Arts, and the Province of British Columbia through the BC
Arts Council and the Book Publishing Tax Credit.

Cover design by Rachel Page
Cover photography by iStock.com

ORCA BOOK PUBLISHERS
www.orcabook.com

Printed and bound in Canada.

19  18  17  16  •  4  3  2  1

*For Marla Albiston*

# The Seattle Public Library
Columbia Branch
Visit us on the Web: www.spl.org

## Checked Out Items 6/11/2019 17:58
## XXXXXXXXX1417

| Item Title | Due Date |
| --- | --- |
| 0010088288161 | 7/2/2019 |
| Across the floor | |
| 0010086723052 | 7/2/2019 |
| Burned | |
| 0010089803893 | 7/2/2019 |
| He who dreams | |

# of Items: 3

**Balance Due: $2.26**

Renewals: 206-386-4190
TeleCirc: 206-386-9015 / 24 hours a day
Online: myaccount.spl.org

Pay your fines/fees online at pay.spl.org

# One

This can't be happening to me. For real, this can't be happening to me. I do a quick check of my surroundings. Coach's office. Smell of sweat and mold. Coach, doing that quiet voice he does when he means business.

Yep.

This is really happening. Oh man.

"—cost us." Coach shakes his head. "We were so close to the win."

I wince. Bad enough that I haven't forgotten my spectacular failure that cost us the football championship. Even worse that today, on the last day of school, it's clear that Coach hasn't forgotten either. "It's not like I meant to have my knee snap," I say.

That moment still gives me nightmares. The final sixty seconds in the game, the end zone in my sight. I could almost feel the cold metal of the trophy in my hands...

And that was my fatal mistake. My attention had shifted. It was enough for the other team's defensive lineman to grab me around the waist and haul me down.

There went my knee, the game, the trophy and the feel of victory.

Coach sighs. "No one ever means to get an injury, Luc."

The first rule in any game—especially when you're a smaller player like me—is never let your opponent see you nervous. I lean back in the metal chair. "So, I don't get on the team next year because I got hurt." I want to say more, to fight and point out that I'm one of his best players. But I keep my mouth shut. My mom's a detective in Vice. She says that silence is often the best way to break a suspect. I press my lips together, even though the words threaten to burst free.

"You were great this year. No one can argue that." His gaze flicks to the papers on his desk.

I brace myself against the disappointment and heartbreak bubbling in me. This is surreal. In my worst nightmares it never occurred to me that Coach would kick me off the team.

I love football.

I *live* football.

Geez, I'd sleep in the end zone if I could.

"You're a shoo-in at tryouts and on the team... on one condition."

I raise an eyebrow and tie an anchor to the hope that's rising like a helium balloon.

"Dance."

"Gesundheit."

"I didn't sneeze."

"Then that's one weird cough."

Coach rolls his eyes. "I mean what I say. It'll be a great supplemental sport for you."

For me, if it doesn't involve sneakers, a uniform, mouthguard, shin pads or a helmet, it's not really a sport.

"Dance is an excellent strengthening activity," Coach says. "Steve McLendon does ballet. If it's good enough for an NFL player, then it should be good enough for E.J. Marshall's defensive lineman."

Gimme me a break. Steve McLendon's 320 pounds. I'm positive his parents don't question anything he does. My parents, on the other hand, will be questioning why I have to join dance when I'm already in a bunch of other sports during the school year.

"Dance will help with your flexibility and strength. Luc, you're one of the best players I've got. I can't risk losing you to an injury. I don't want to lose a championship because you hurt yourself. Dance will give you that extra conditioning you need."

I can't argue with his reasoning. I'm not averse to doing what's necessary to stay on the team. When Coach said he didn't think I had good lung strength, I joined track and field to build endurance. Then I joined swim for stamina, and soccer for footwork. But dance?

"Can't I do something else? What about extra swimming classes?" I'm leaning forward in the chair. Bad move. It transmits emotions I want to keep private. I lean back and wait for his answer.

Coach ponders. The chair rattles as he straightens. "No, dance is best." He takes a breath. "Unless you think you can't do it?"

"That's not the point. Point is, I don't think you can force me to do this."

"You're right. It's your choice. Just like it's my choice who I allow on the team next year." He gives me a stare. "What's it going to be?"

*   *   *

That night Dad and I sit down at the computer and go through the summer dance classes. The spicy scent of *bobotie*, a curried shepherd's pie from Mom's home country, South Africa, lingers in the air.

"I can't believe Coach is making you do this." Dad scowls as he scrolls through the online list. The glow of the computer screen lights his face and reveals his irritation. His face is almost as red as his hair.

"Me neither."

"He told you to join track and field to build endurance, and you did. Then it was soccer. Then swimming." He turns his scowl my way. "How many more sports are you supposed to take part in before this guy is happy?"

"Coach says it'll make me a better player."

"Coach always says that." Dad sighs. "And look at this." He waves his hand at the computer screen. "Look at the cost and the time. How are you supposed to help me this summer?"

Oh man. "I hadn't thought of that."

"Well, think about it. 'Cause it's your sport and your social life on the line."

The deal in the family is that my parents pay for school supplies—books, pens, computers and stuff like that—as well as most of my sports fees, housing and food. Everything else—clothes, 10 percent of the fees for sports teams, money to hang out with friends—comes out of my pocket. Plus, 10 percent of my wages has to go to my savings account. And all of that means working with Dad's landscaping company in the summer.

"We've got a ton of new clients. Plus the long-time clients too. What about Mrs. O'Connor?" Dad takes his hands from the keyboard and turns to me. "Are you going to give her up?"

No way. I really like Mrs. O'Connor and her family. She's got triplets—boys—who're a total riot, and her husband is in the military. Helping them is my way of saying thanks for his service and their sacrifice. "I'll still mow Mrs. O'Connor's lawn. It'll be fine."

"That's what you think, huh?" Dad gives me a pitying look and turns back to the computer. "All these studios are running day-long classes. And those classes run three weeks. You do the math on how much money both you and I are about to lose while you learn how to pirouette."

I read over his shoulder. "I can't take any of those classes anyway. Coach says I only have to do contemporary dance. These classes are a full day, with a bunch of different styles." I give his shoulder a gentle shove.

He takes the hint and gets up.

Sitting down, I grab the mouse and keyboard and start a new search.

"I'm not hiring a new guy." He's on repeat mode of his rant. "You know the clients, know what they like. Dance or no dance, I expect you to work."

"Yes, sir!" I salute him.

His lips quirk. "Don't be a smart aleck. Football costs money. A lot of money. So do all the other sports you're doing. You have to do your part. And that means mowing lawns."

"Look, Coach said to take contemporary dance. It's not like it's going to take all summer. I promise, it'll be fine."

"What's going on?" Mom comes into the room. She has a plate of fruit in her hand and offers me a slice of pineapple.

"Dad's reading me the riot act about taking dance this summer." I take a bite of the pineapple.

"I hope you're listening. If we have to hire someone to take your place—" Her voice is calm, and if she's irritated, her dark skin hides the evidence.

"Geez."

"Don't 'geez' me, young man. You have responsibilities—"

"I've heard this already. Don't worry, okay? It'll be fine. But for your lack of maternal support"—I grab the plate from Mom—"you'll lose your fruit."

"Hey!"

I bite into an apple. "Anyway, it won't be that bad."

"Really?" Mom hikes an eyebrow and takes back her plate. "You don't think it'll interfere with your work for your dad? And how do you plan on getting to those classes?"

"The truck—" Oops.

"My truck?"

If her eyebrow goes any higher, it's going to need its own zip code. "Uh..."

She sighs. "I suppose I can catch a ride with your dad sometimes...but Thursdays I have to have the car. Got it?"

I nod and go back to working the computer screen. I'm trying to sign up before my parents change their minds, but most of these classes run all day and have a variety of dance styles. Isn't there anything—"Here we go. Madison Studio. They have a bunch of classes focused on one style. Contemporary is Tuesday and Thursday from ten to one."

"That's three hours you're missing of work. Twice a week. Six hours total."

Trust Dad to point out the obvious. "Yeah, but I'll make it up. Instead of working till four, I'll work until seven."

"You sure you want to do this?" asks Mom.

"Coach said it's this or not be on the team."

"But you're a great player." She keeps pushing. "We can get you in another league. Or worse comes to worst, put you in another school."

9

No. No way. Football rises and falls on the strength of the team, and the strength of the team depends on how well the members connect. My team's amazing. We have each other's backs, on the field and off. Plus, Coach is the best in the city. No way am I letting down my friends, my coach or myself. "I promise, it'll be fine. Let me sign up, okay?"

My parents exchange a long look, and then Dad nods.

Mom drops a kiss on the top of my forehead and stands behind me as we sign me up for class.

Dad presses *Enter*, and it's done.

I'm about to become a dancer.

# Two

I open my eyes and blink. Something's off. It tickles the back of my brain. Frowning, I sit up and try to figure out what's wrong. Dance class today, but that's annoying, not weird. The house is quiet. Mom and Dad are at work. I glance at my phone, and it takes me a second to register the time. Nine o'clock. I should've been up by seven thirty.

Geez, I've totally slept in! I scramble to get out of bed, get caught in the sheets, fall and land awkwardly and painfully on the floor. By the time I'm dressed and out the door, I've made up some of the lost time, but I'm still ten minutes behind schedule. Mom and Dad will kill me if I get a speeding ticket, but I figure doing five over the limit isn't so bad.

\*   \*   \*

I manage to get to the studio on schedule. My heart is pounding by the time I pull into the parking lot. Not a good pounding, like when I step on the field. The bad kind of pounding, like when I have to get up and do a presentation in front of class. I'm trying to think of being here as a challenge. I remind myself that this is what's keeping me on the team and getting me that football scholarship. That'll get me an education, and *that* will get me a future. But all I can think about is the work I'm missing and how long my days are going to be since I'll have to make up those hours. I feel uncomfortable and out of place. Dance isn't remotely like anything I've ever done before.

No field.

No padding.

No mouthguards.

There's nothing in the uniform I'm wearing—stretchy black pants, sleeveless shirt—that makes me feel like I'm stepping into a familiar arena. I kill the engine and get out of the trunk. The morning sun is already noonday hot. I'm totally sweating. I'll be drenched before I hit the entrance. I take a shallow breath and head to the glass doors. A couple of girls push past me and toss a smile my way. I'm too ticked at Coach, too hot, too anxious and too annoyed at this total waste of time, to smile back.

They glance at each other, shrug and go inside.

I try to follow. Only, I can't make my feet move. I *want* to make them move, but they won't do anything.

Unlike my armpits. Those suckers are in overdrive. I'm sweating through my antiperspirant. I tighten my grip on my bag with one hand. Before my brain can have any second, third or fourth thoughts, I open the door and step inside. There's a second of relief as the air-conditioning hits. Then I take in the room. Mirrors on the wall, polished hardwood floors, lots of sun from the window. And kids. There's about fifteen of them, including me.

Thirteen of them are girls.

If my buddy Tim was here, he'd go bananas at the ratio. Tim's all about the girls. I drop my bag by the other bags. Most of the kids are warming up. They look like they're doing impressions of pretzels. A couple of them are doing knee bends by a stretch bar. Some are on the floor doing the splits, and a couple are balancing on one leg and doing some kind of standing split.

In the back of my brain, an alarm starts to sound. I'd figured the class would all be rookies like me, learning steps and easy dance routines. But the way these kids are stretching says they have a background in dance or gymnastics.

In football, I've lost whatever flexibility I ever had. I can do short, sharp moves, but I don't think the dance instructor will have us doing any routines where I get to tackle someone. And now I'm surrounded by kids who have no problems touching their toes. How am I going to keep up once class starts?

Oh man, am I in trouble.

What has Coach gotten me into?

Check that question.

What have *I* gotten myself into?

\* \* \*

The kids are in the center of the dance floor, hanging out and chatting. I stand at the edge of the group and look at the one other guy in the class. We're wearing the same outfit. The only difference?

He looks comfortable, and I feel completely exposed. I glance at my watch. It's a couple minutes after ten. Where's the instructor? Man, I lost five pounds in sweat trying to get here on time, and the instructor's taking his sweet time. If class runs late, then the lawn mowing will run late. I swallow the groan rising in my throat, but my irritation kicks up another notch.

"Hey."

"Hey," I say back to the girl approaching me. Tim would go nuts for her. She's Asian and tiny, with strong shoulders and amazing biceps.

"I'm Brittney," she says. "Two *t*'s, one *n*, one *e*."

Wow. Okay. "Uh, I'm Luc. One *l*, one *u*, one *c*."

Her eyebrows go up. "Is that short for Lukas, Lucius or something really exotic, like Lucentio?"

I take another glance at the clock on the wall. *Where's the instructor?*

"Don't tell," says the guy as he approaches us.

He's tall and thin, with coloring a little darker than mine. Years of playing football make me gauge him from the perspective of either an opponent or member of my team. I could tackle him in a scrimmage, but his long legs say I'd be running for days trying to catch him.

"Negotiate," he continues. "Tell her you'll give her your middle name in return for her Chinese name."

This makes Brittney roll her eyes. "Ignore him," she says. "Jesse has been after me since kindergarten to give it up." She pokes him in the chest. "Not happening, buddy."

"C'mon," Jesse says. "I'll tell you my full name."

That gets another eye roll. Brittney takes my hand and pulls me away. "Let me introduce you to everyone."

I don't want to be dragged anywhere, but she's stronger than she looks, and I follow.

Brittney must be a museum tour guide in training, because she gives me entire histories on everyone. She's about three kids in before she stops to take a breath, and I jump in. "Where's the instructor?"

"Peter?" Her nose crinkles. "Maybe he's caught in traffic."

I take a step back, but Brittney says, "Where are you going? Don't you want to meet everyone?"

"I have friends, thanks." It comes out ruder than I mean, but I'm in no mood to say sorry. I want the class to start so it can end.

She flinches and shoots Jesse a *What now?* look.

"Come on, bro," says Jesse. "She's just trying to welcome you."

"I feel real welcomed, okay? Like we've been friends forever." Wow. That *really* sounds rude, but for real, I don't want friends, I don't want life histories. I'm like a prisoner. I want to keep my head down, do my time and get out when my sentence is over.

Jesse tosses a frown my way, then shrugs at Brittney and waves her over.

I take another look at the clock. Ten after. Great. Just great. I head back to my bag and sit down. I'm fuming. Either it shows on my face or my run-in with Brittney and Jesse has gone viral, because the rest of the kids aren't coming near me.

I pull my knees to my chest and half listen, half watch what's going on. From what I gather, they all seem to know each other, either from school or other dance classes. None of them have a contemporary-dance background, but all of them have done some kind of dance: Afro-jazz, ballet, tap. I'd figured the class would be newbies like me.

Still, I'm not super worried. Dance may have different steps and moves, but at its core, it's movement. I'm an athlete. I'm in a bunch of organized sports, plus gym, street hockey and stuff. I'm positive I'll be able to pick up contemporary with no problem. If the instructor would show up. I watch the minute hand move toward the number five on the clock face and get madder with every passing second.

\* \* \*

"I see familiar faces," the instructor says when he finally shows up. He's tall and slim, with dark hair pulled into a ponytail.

Brittney was right—he was caught in traffic. It's hypocritical for me to be ticked off that he's late, considering my own mad rush to get here on time. But I can't help the irritation that keeps swimming to the surface.

The instructor focuses on me. "And I see some unfamiliar faces. I'm Peter—"

The kids gather around him in a semicircle. I hang back. Way back.

"—and I'll be your instructor." The way he says it sounds more like he's threatening us than introducing himself.

"This is a beginner contemporary class, so don't worry." His smile doesn't reach his eyes. "I won't work you too hard."

The nervous laughter among the kids says they know Peter is a tough instructor.

That's fine by me. I'm up for the challenge. Peter's gaze hasn't left me. It's like he's doing a combination CT scan, X-ray and MRI, gauging my athleticism and ability.

I get the distinct feeling I've failed his first assessment.

He looks away. "Most of you have worked with me before." His gaze flicks back to me. "And those who are new to the program will learn to be fast learners."

When he's done taking attendance, he tells us to get into formation.

I watch for a second and realize he's asking us to form three lines of five in a row. I grab a spot in the middle row, in the middle of the line.

We lock gazes, and he gives me a small nod.

I've moved from an F grade to a D-minus.

Maybe this won't be so bad.

# Three

"Okay, folks." Peter claps his hands. "We'll do a warm-up to get your blood flowing, your body stretched, and then we'll move across the floor."

Move across the floor? Man, I know he's using English words, but he may as well be speaking ancient Egyptian.

He heads to the sound dock and punches a button. Coldplay's "A Sky Full of Stars" begins. At first I'm sort of keeping up. Shoulder rolls, torso twists. I feel a rush of pride when he moves to hip rolls and I can actually, sort of, kind of do them. But five minutes in, I don't know what's going on or how to keep up.

Peter's saying things like, "Let's move through demi-plié."

My brain scrolls for what a demi-plié might be, but the darn thing sounds like dessert. *Waiter, I'll have a demi-plié and an Earl Grey tea. Thanks.*

A quick glance at Brittney says that whatever I'm doing, it's not a plié. I'm not even sure what I'm doing can be classified as a dance move. I rush to catch up, to do what she's doing, but Peter says, "Great. Now grand plié..."

Oh man. I'm so lost. I stand there for a minute, watching so I can copy.

Jesse looks over at me, then keeps going.

I do what he does. Sort of.

"Demi-plié, left, swing up and down, then drop down into a right lunge."

It's getting harder to keep up, and ten minutes in, when he says, "Battement with the left," I'm lost.

I have no clue what's going on. The only reason I figure out it's some kind of kick is 'cause when I almost get a heel to the shin, courtesy of the kid next to me.

"Luc, watch your space!"

I get the gist of the command and skitter out of the way. Then I do my best to battement. And almost pull a muscle.

Peter's not helping. "Luc! Push your range of motion."

Man, is he kidding? Tossing out foreign words, thinking I'm going to catch on and do it perfectly? This guy could make Genghis Khan's kid cry.

Coldplay's given way to Marvin Gaye. Around me, the kids are moving in sync with Peter's commands. They're like human versions of a flock of starlings. Everyone's swaying and moving in sync with each other and the music. They bend in unison, rise as one. This may be basic stuff to them, stretching and warm-up, but it looks like dance to me.

Worst of all, with mirrors on three walls, I have an almost 360-degree view of myself. If they're starlings, then I'm a turkey in the flock.

Half an hour in, Peter tells us to grab some water and take five. My muscles are shaking, and I can barely stand. I stifle a groan when he says, "After the break, we'll really move across the floor."

"What were we doing for the last hour?" I grumble to myself.

"I don't know what you were doing," says Jesse as he walks by, "but it looked like Peter was mopping the floor with you."

Brittney jerks her thumb toward the door, ignores me and talks to Jesse. "You wanna grab some water and sit outside for a bit?"

He nods, and they walk off.

I go to my bag, grab my water bottle and take three big gulps before coming up for air. I want to sit down. Correction. I want to collapse on the floor, but my brain says that if I do, I may never stand again.

*   *   *

"Thanks for coming back so quickly," says Peter when he calls us back from break. "We'll work on a few different sets of choreography over the next few weeks. Because you're beginners, we'll do an easy routine."

Easy for them, maybe. But I'm starting to feel like a six-year-old doing university math.

"First, I'm going to show you what you can accomplish if you train hard and practice even harder." He steps away from us, cues the music and takes a stance.

I don't know what I was expecting. Classical music, maybe, and a lot of leaping and jumping.

Instead, Sam Smith's "Not in That Way" pours through the speakers. Peter puts his hands to his chest, then lets them drop as he sinks to his knees.

Peter's not a big guy. But he seems to take over the studio...seems *bigger* than the studio, and he seems to grow with every breath he takes. He stretches toward the group, and I swear, his hands lengthen, his fingers grow longer, until I'm sure he could touch us even though we are at least two feet away.

I may not like dance, but I'll admit, he's got my attention. And I'm not the only one. A bunch of kids, Jesse and Brittney included, have their phones out and are videoing him.

"Look at his extensions," murmurs Jesse.

"Forget the extension," replies Brittney. "Look at the height in his jumps."

"What about the control in his turns?"

I zone out as they continue to talk about Peter's fluidity of movement and expression. I'm too busy watching and trying to figure out what he's doing and how I can mimic it. I don't know what this "across the floor" thing is, but my competitive edge kicks in.

Jesse was right. Peter mopped the floor with me during the first half of the class.

No way am I letting him do it to me for the rest of these sessions.

* * *

When the last note of the music fades away, Peter moves from his spot in the center of the dance floor and claps his hands. "Okay, people, let's keep going."

The kids take spots around the room, their backs to the wall. I do the same.

"Let's do some side falls and triplets," says Peter. He crosses the length of the studio and comes to a stop by me. "Luc, I'm going to break this down for you step by step, okay?"

I feel the heat creeping into my cheeks at him singling me out, but I keep eye contact with him and nod.

"Good. Okay. For the rest of you, it won't hurt to pay attention to the breakdown too. We'll start with one of the foundational moves in contemporary dance. Triplets are a core step when you're traveling across the floor space."

He straightens, moves his arms out so they're thirty degrees from his body. "Start with your right foot back, spiral your body left. Rotate to the right, relevé right, relevé left, plié right, relevé left, relevé right, plié left, then step right, step left into preparation for ballet fourth position, prep for a double pirouette—yes, double; challenge yourself—and back to start."

He looks around. "Any questions?"

Everyone seems to understand, including me. I may not understand the terms, but I get the movement. Face left, turn right, go on my tiptoes with my right foot, then my left, bend my knees, do another tiptoe walk, turn a couple of times. Yeah, I got this.

"Great. Let's go."

I'm not sure why, but instead of doing the formation from this morning, the class forms two lines at the side of the room. Since there's an uneven number, there's no one across from me in the second line. I don't know if that's good or bad. And I doubly don't know what's going on, so I'm glad I'm the last to go.

"Okay." Peter cues the music. "Five, six, five, six, seven, eight."

The two kids at the front of the lines move into the open dance space and repeat what Peter did with the triple-step thing. Only they're doing it way faster than he did. Faster than I think I can do.

Then it hits me.

They're doing it two by two.

I'll be alone on the dance floor in front of everyone when my turn comes.

Oh man.

# Four

The class does the triple-step thing in twos, and even though they're not as polished as Peter—except maybe Jesse and Brittney—they're decent.

Peter looks my way.

My mouth goes dry.

"Five, six," he counts.

And my brain goes blank. I can't remember what the steps were.

"Five, six—"

Something about a plié and a reveler. Maybe. No, wait, a reveler is some kind of a partygoer. Oh man. I'm in trouble.

"—seven, eight."

My feet won't move. And I think I've forgotten how to breathe.

"Try again, Luc. Five, six—"

"I can't remember the steps," I blurt out and feel my face go hot.

Jesse ducks his head and hides his laughter behind his hand.

"Start with your right foot back, spiral your body left," Peter says. "Rotate to the right, relevé right, relevé left, plié right, relevé left, relevé right, plié left. Then step right, step left into preparation for ballet fourth position, prep for a double pirouette and back to start."

"Uh—"

"Okay, no problem." Peter takes a spot opposite me. "Follow me, okay?"

I nod and hope I don't throw up. This has never happened to me before. I've always been able to get the play.

"Five, six, five, six, seven, eight…"

Peter leaps into motion, and I follow. He's smooth, graceful. In the mirror, I see my reflection. Smooth and graceful doesn't describe me.

I look more like a lumbering caveman wondering what happened to my cave.

Peter makes the group run through the steps a couple more times, then says, "Let's move on to chaînés."

He shows us what it is—and this time I know I can nail it. It's just spinning from one end of the room to the other. I've been doing that since I was four.

We all take our spots. Peter pairs me with Brittney, and Jesse is on his own. I watch as the others take their turn. In my head, I keep repeating what I'm supposed to do: spin, spin, spin.

Peter gives the count, and I'm set. "Five, six, seven, eight."

I'm spinning in time with the music, smooth, effortless, easy—until I smack into something soft. There's a tangle of legs and arms, and I find myself on the floor with Brittney.

She shoves me away. "Learn how to spot, dude!"

I don't know what that is and there's no time to ask. Peter is telling us to clear the floor so we can move on with the class. I'd say this day can't get any worse, but somehow I think I'm about to be proven wrong.

"Great work, guys! I thought I would take it slow with you, but it looks like everyone's keeping up." He doesn't look at me when he says this. "Let's really start having some fun with across the floor."

Why do I feel like *fun* is code for "I'm about to make this harder?" The class moves to the walls while Peter takes a position at one end of the room. "Our next across the floor will be ball-change fan kick, chaîné, chaîné, roll to the ground—do it with a hip roll—to standing position, then repeat." He straightens up, shoulders back. "So ball-change right to left in plié on one, and fan-kick your right leg on count two." He does a class-wide glance and makes eye contact with each of us. "Make sure to really pull up in your thigh on the supporting leg, and be on a nice strong relevé. Step onto the fanning leg—make sure to step onto a straight leg—and chaîné on three and four."

I'm trying to match his movement with his words, but my brain's spinning and most of me is freaking out over the fan kick. Peter's got wicked extension and flexibility. I think I'm going to pull something in my thigh and hips if I try to kick that high and then spin my leg like a fan.

31

"Let me see a nice tight first position with your feet on your turns, and a strong, round first position with your arms. On count five, make sure your hips are square to the front, and step out with your right leg. Then spiral to the floor as you put your left hip down on six, roll around on your bum to stand up on your left leg on seven, and keep turning around to face the front on eight, and you're ready to start again." He claps his hands. "First two, get ready to go."

Jesse and Brittney step up.

Peter counts them in. "Five, six, five, six, seven, eight..."

By the time it's my turn, I'm sure I've sweated through my antiperspirant now, and the thought of lifting my stinky arms isn't thrilling. Even less exciting is knowing I have to perform in front of a bunch of kids I don't know and do a set of dance steps I can't remember.

"I'll go with you," says Peter.

I croak out something that sounds like, "Okay."

He counts us in, and then he steps onto the dance floor.

I stare at his feet.

"Hands up, Luc!"

My hands shoot into the air like I'm in a stickup. The class laughs, and I drop and extend them outward instead of upward. I try to do the ball change, shift my weight to my right leg, then the left, then cross my right leg in front. The worst part is catching my reflection in the mirror. I look like a bear that's had too many overripe berries and is trying to find a warm place to nap.

"Next time, Luc," says Peter as we reach the other side, "you need to be on the ball of your left foot, then cross your right leg over with the foot of your supporting leg turned out."

I nod, fake like I understand what he says and make a mental note to watch the kids' feet when we do it again. Jesse and Brittney begin the second run-through, and I stand in the back, catching my breath and pretending I didn't pull something in my thigh trying to do the fan kick. But the muscle's pinging, and so is the toe I stubbed when I tried to do the ball change.

Peter continues, but it only gets worse. My entire knowledge of dance is the funky chicken and some lame thing my mom taught me called the Macarena. I'm so far behind the rest of the kids it's not even funny. And the worst part is that all the sports I've done aren't doing anything to help me keep up. I've never been this lost in anything involving physical movement. I can't help but wonder, If this is the first—and probably the easiest—class, how am I supposed to survive the rest of the sessions?

*   *   *

After the class ends, Peter calls out my name. "Luc, hang back." He wipes his face with a black towel, then tosses it on his bag.

He waits until the studio's clear, then asks, "Why are you here?"

I tell him my story.

"Football player," he grunts. "That explains the body movements."

I'm not sure if he's making an observation or taking a shot, so I stay quiet. But something must show on my face, because he says, "No foul intended. You're like my mom."

Okay, how is *that* not a slam?

"She wanted to play piano after she retired from working as an executive assistant. Lots of typing in her work." He mimes the action. "She'd spent years holding her hands a certain way, but to play a piano, your hand positions are completely different. It was really hard for her to learn how to hold her hands."

I don't understand. "Is there something wrong with my hands?"

"Kid, there's something wrong with everything you're doing. You don't even stand correctly. You're clunky and awkward and you're a menace to the other dancers."

That makes me wince.

"I'm not trying to be mean, but I'm asking if this is really something you need to do."

"If I want to stay on the football team, I do."

"What about yoga?"

"Coach said dance."

"Flexibility training?"

"Isn't that dancing?"

That makes him crack a smile. "Touché. I'm not trying to be a jerk, but you saw these guys today. They may not know contemporary dance—"

"But they know dance."

"They're catching the choreography fast, which means I can increase the complexity..." He trails off.

"You don't think I can keep up."

"How do *you* think you did today?"

Ouch. I don't say anything.

"Maybe you can take another class?"

"This is the only one being offered this summer," I say. "I have to get it done or I don't get to try out."

Peter's expression is part sympathy, part *Not my problem, kid.* "I'm not telling you to drop out, but I am telling you what's going to happen in the next class. It's not fair to hold the entire class back for you—"

"I'm not asking you to!"

"But it's not fair to push you so far outside your abilities. You could really hurt yourself."

Great. Coach says to take dance so I don't hurt myself. Peter says to stop dancing before I hurt myself.

"I empathize with your situation, but I have fourteen other kids to think of. I'm not holding back for you." Peter packs up his things and walks out the door.

I watch him walk away, knowing he's not wrong. I'd be ticked if Coach started running baby plays for some rookie. I've never been the one who couldn't keep up. I have a sudden empathy for all the guys who got cut from the team. And I'm ashamed for judging how hard they did—or didn't—work to run the plays. I grab my bag and head out the door.

# Five

I t's almost quarter to two by the time I'm back on the road, and I'm scrambling—again—to make up for lost time. I get to the first house on my schedule, the O'Connors. As soon as I pull the truck into the driveway and cut the engine, the O'Connors Three are out the door. Braden, Dale and Tom. Four-year-old triplets with awesome fire-red hair and brown eyes.

I climb out of the seat and feel every movement. All the sitting has made my muscles cramp up and tightened my back. The truck door creaks as I begin to close it. Then again, maybe that's the sound my knees make as I try to straighten up.

"Luc! You're here!" Dale does an excited lap around my legs as I slam the door shut.

"You're late." Tom holds up his left hand, a too-big watch dangling from his wrist.

"I am?" I give him a wide-eyed gaze. "How late am I?"

He looks at the watch. "You were supposed to be here at the three. Now it's at the six."

I stifle my laugh. Tom's obviously learning how to tell time, and I don't want to point out he's mixing up his numbers. "Gee, what time does that mean?"

He glares at me. "I said. At the six!"

I hide my smile.

Their mom comes running out. "Luc, I'm so sorry! Guys! Back in the house, now!"

"But we have to help Luc," says Dale. "He has to do all the bagging." He gives his mom a stern look. "We always help him."

Mrs. O'Connor herds them back inside. "Sorry about that."

"It's no problem. I like them." I turn—slowing down as my back twinges—and carefully lift the lawn mower to the ground. Usually this isn't a big deal, but thanks to my dance class, my biceps are shaking with the weight of the equipment.

"Was the traffic bad?"

I wince. "I'm sorry about being late." I give her the lowdown on the dance classes.

"Wow, Coach is really laying it on the line with you, huh?"

"Yeah." I make sure the lawn mower's secure, then shut the truck's tailgate. "But I'll do anything he says to stay in football."

"It's nice he's looking out for you and trying to prevent you from getting hurt."

"Yeah, I'd rather get sturdier equipment."

She laughs. "It won't be so bad." Looking over her shoulder, she notices the kids, pressed up against the living-room window. "I'll keep the triple terrors out of your hair."

That would help me with the schedule. I'm supposed to meet Dad and another crew at four o'clock to do the grounds at the museum. But the O'Connor boys always help me bag the cut grass, and I can imagine their faces if their mom tells them that they have to stay inside. "It's okay," I tell her. "They always help, and I don't mind."

"Well, if they're with you...I could use the time to get some stuff done."

I can almost see her weighing the pros and cons in her head.

"It's not fair to you, Luc—"

"Honestly, I don't mind."

"Well, if you're okay—"

"I'll tap on the patio door when I'm ready."

She smiles. "You're a good kid, Luc. It makes the boys' day when you come around."

"Mine too," I say, smiling.

She heads inside, and I push the mower toward the backyard. The gentle slope of their driveway feels like Mount Everest. By the time I get to the backyard, my upper arms are letting me know they'd like me to get a lighter mower. My legs would like me to get a lawn mower I can sit on to drive. Man. Who knew dance—even a beginner's class—could be that hard on your muscles? I start the engine and take the mower to the lawn.

Usually, the O'Connors' yard takes me a half hour to do. But I'm moving slower, and the workout from this morning is making it harder, and it's adding time. I can't welch on my promise to the boys, so I tap on the patio door when I'm finished mowing. They tumble out.

Tom directs the team. Braden and Dale hold open the garbage bag, and I shake in the clippings. I always keep a hand on the bag to help steady it. But today I'm the one who isn't quite steady. It's hard to balance the lawn-mower bag in one hand and the garbage bag in the other, but I finally get it all done.

I send the kids back inside so I can edge the lawn, and then I pack up. The boys race back out as I'm struggling to heft the lawn mower onto the truck bed.

"When are you coming back again?"

"Next time can I lift the bag?"

"Are you going to be late again?"

Now I'm struggling to stay patient with them, lift the lawn mower and do both in the blazing sun when I'm sore and tired. I corral the kids back to the house, get in the truck and check the clock. Time's not on my side, which means no stopping for anything to eat before the next job. I do a quick check of my water bottle. Empty. Great.

I do my best to pick up my pace, but as the day drags on, I'm moving slower and everything is taking longer. The sun feels too hot. The grass pieces that fly out from the weed whacker hit me like knives. The traffic's too slow. And I'm not fast enough. It's almost five when I get to the museum grounds, and I arrive in time to see the guys loading up for the day.

One of the guys from Dad's crew spots me. "Hey, thanks for showing up, princess. Did the servants not wake you in time?" He catches the look on my face, and his grin drops. "Whoa, sorry, Luc. I was joshin'. You okay?"

"Yeah, it's been a bad day," I say.

"Not just for you." Dad strides up. "An hour late? You better not blame traffic, because I know for a fact there were no holdups on your routes."

"I'm not blaming the traffic."

"It was the class, wasn't it?"

"It ran a little late this one time—"

"Luc, what did I tell you about the classes and your responsibility to this family?"

"Look, I'm sorry, okay? The class was late, and then I had the O'Connors, and you know the kids like to help me—"

Dad's eyebrows go up. "Are you blaming your tardiness on a bunch of toddlers?"

"No, it's..." I take a breath. "I had my butt handed to me today in class, okay? I couldn't keep up. It's nothing like I thought it would be.

43

Football, we do some warm-ups, then play. In three hours of dance, two and a half hours were warm-ups and exercises. Hardly any dancing. Not that it would have mattered. I sucked at everything."

Dad sighs. "You don't *need* this. Let me talk to Coach in fall and—"

"I don't want to quit."

"But on your first day, you're letting me down. You're not only part of a football team, son, you're part of my team and your mom's. We have to be able to count on you."

"I know. I was caught off guard today. But I know the warm-up now and the across-the-floor stuff, and I'm sure I'll catch on to the choreo. Give me a month. If I can't make it work, then I'll quit and mow lawns."

"I can't afford to give you a month," he says. "You've got two weeks to make this work or you cut out dance. Deal?"

What else can I say? "Deal."

* * *

The next morning my alarm goes off forty-five minutes earlier than normal. That was on purpose. After yesterday's dismal performance at dance class, I'm not about to get schooled again. I figure forty-five minutes of practice this morning, a half hour around lunch and an hour after dinner will help me remember the warm-ups and help me to look more like the studio kids and less like a guy trying to do the funky chicken.

The alarm's still buzzing, and I start to roll over to shut it off. I get a millisecond into the roll before my body starts screaming. I've heard about being sore the day after, but this is sore on steroids. I stop moving, breathe and then try again. The pain slices through me. My back, my neck, my hips, my arms. I think it even hurts to blink. Groaning, I manage to sit up and shut off the alarm. But after that, all I can do is sit. And breathe. Shallowly breathe.

I'm moving like a ninety-year-old man. Check that. A 100-year-old would move faster than me. I drag myself through my morning routine. Forget about practicing anything today. I'll be lucky to walk upright! And the only good thing I can say about getting up earlier is that it lets me get out the door on time.

The bright side of today is that on Wednesdays I do bigger jobs, like school fields and grounds on some of the factories around town, which means spending the day with Tim. And using riding mowers. I pick him up in front of his house, where he's got a travel cup of coffee in each hand.

"Hey, bud." He climbs in the cab and holds out one of the mugs.

I'm too sore to reach for it and too proud to tell him why, so I say, "Stick it in the cup holder for now."

He does, and we head to our first job. I'm having trouble shoulder-checking because of my neck. Tim notices. "Whoa. What's going on with you?"

"Oh, uh, just sore."

"It's a little early for football training. We got out of classes last week."

"Uh, yeah, it's good to stay in shape. You know, start ready instead of get ready."

He nods. "So what's the training you're doing? Maybe I should tag along?" He pats his stomach. "With summer and ice cream, it won't hurt me to stay in shape."

I go silent.

Tim waits as I pull up to a stop sign, then waits some more as I go straight.

"So?" he finally asks. "What's the training?"

"Uh—"

"You already said that."

"It's dance," I blurt out.

There's dead silence.

"Dance?" Tim repeats. "Like hip-hop aerobics?"

*I wish.* "More like contemporary dance."

"What's that?"

"It's kind of like ballet."

Tim lets out a whoop. "Ballet? Ballet? You're lacing up with ribbons and tights? Yo, dude, tell me I can come and take photos."

"Shut up."

"For real? You're doing dance? Dude, why?"

"'Cause Coach said."

"Hey, for real?" The laughter's gone. If Coach says something, we all take it seriously. "Dance? Why?"

I tell him about the injuries and Coach's theory of dance helping to strengthen my muscles.

"A bunch of the pros do it," says Tim. "And Coach isn't wrong. You got what it takes to go to the NFL. No one wants to see that dream die out in freshman year because of a torn ACL." He stops, watches me for a bit. "But are you messing with me? Did dance class really leave you in this sorry condition?"

"Man, it hurts to blink."

That gets him laughing again.

The day isn't so bad. With Tim helping out, I'm able to stay on schedule and get help lifting the mowers up and down. Sure, he makes me pay for it with a bunch of ballet jokes and questions about what size my tutu is, but he's also the angel on my shoulder.

"Is it totally kicking your butt?" he asks when we break for lunch. We take a spot in the shade on the field of the elementary school we've just mowed.

I nod. Half-nod. I'm not as sore as I was this morning, but I'm nowhere near fighting shape. "I hate to admit it, but it's the hardest thing I've ever done."

"Even with the relays Coach makes us do?"

"That stuff's cardio, and it's brutal. But this dancing thing is cardio plus balance. And control." I swallow my embarrassment and tell him about spinning into Brittney.

"Hold up." He pulls out his phone. "I gotta text that to the guys."

"Come on. Let this be between us."

"No way. This is treasure. Like the King Tut of awesome stories. It's my duty to share it with the team."

A couple of minutes later my cell lights up with jokes. I hold it up so Tim can see the screen. "I'll remember this if you ever need a kidney or a lung."

He slaps me on the back, then laughs when I howl in pain.

"Man up," he says. "Coach says it'll help, then it'll help. And do it right. You gonna practice when you get home?"

"I wanted to, but I'm sore."

"If you don't move, it'll only get worse." He jumps up from the ground, dusts the sandwich crumbs from his hands. "Come on. No one's around—show me some of the choreography. I'll do it with you."

"Seriously?"

"Yeah, there's no one around. It's only us. But if you video me and post anything, I'm going to take one of those lungs, like, now."

"I can't really remember anything. Peter kept talking about staying fluid and in constant motion—"

"Are you a dancer or an ocean?"

"Right now, I'm neither." The choreography was only fifteen minutes of the entire class, and I know there were some kicks and steps and bends, but the order and how to do them is beyond me. "I really can't remember anything."

"What about the warm-up?"

"Yeah, I remember some of it."

"Let's do it."

"Okay, boss." I get up and take him through what I can remember of the warm-up. It's slow going, both trying to remember what the exercises were and how to do them, but it feels good to have Tim on my side. And when the end of the day comes, I'm glad I did my mini workout at lunch. It's fresh in my mind, and after dinner I do another run-through. I'm sure I look like a headless chicken, but I don't care. At least I have the warm-ups in my head. Let Peter try and mop anything with me tomorrow.

# Six

Either the walking while mowing helped stretch and loosen my muscles or I can't get any more sore, because when I wake up, I'm not at the same levels of "ow" as yesterday. And I've gotten up with enough time to get to the studio early. I'm going to go through the warm-up and floor work before the kids and Peter come in. No way am I going to be the first voted off the island today!

I jog-limp upstairs and spy a note taped to the coffeemaker.

*LUC. WORK AT 1:30. YOU'RE LATE, YOU'RE DOCKED. LOVE YOU, DAD.*

I snort at the *LOVE YOU, DAD*. Yeah. Totally feeling the fatherly affection. I down some coffee, grab some toast, then hop in the shower and finish getting ready. Ten minutes ahead of schedule, I head to the front door to grab the keys from the ring and get out of the house.

But the keys aren't there.

Stupidly I stare at the line of key hooks, hoping the keys will magically reappear. They don't. I'm not panicking. I'm ahead of schedule, right? I double back to check my bedroom. Still no keys. Bracing myself for a lecture on my lack of responsibility, I bite the Mom bullet and call her at the station.

"Mom," I say when she picks up. "Do you know what I did with the car keys?"

"Luc, it's Thursday."

I need keys and she's giving me a calendar lesson? "Uh, yeah, and tomorrow's Friday."

"Honey, it's Thursday. I have the keys because—"

"You have the car on Thursdays." I groan. "I totally forgot." Yikes! I have to take the bus. I babble a quick goodbye, then hang up and open the transit app.

Oh man. I've got less than three minutes to get to the stop. I stumble out the door, lock it, sprint for the bus—and get there just as the driver's pulling away from the curb. Lucky for me, he's a nice guy and stops. I get in, pay and grab the first seat I see. My legs are aching from the sudden burst of exercise, my arms are throbbing. I think my back is going to do the physically impossible and break itself free of my body. I'm hoping that by the time I reach the studio, I'll be okay and this won't cost me when class time arrives. I pop in my earbuds, close my eyes and mentally go through the warm-up and across-the-floor stuff. Even if I'm not 100 percent physically speaking, I'm going to make sure I'm in the right head space.

I get to the studio with a couple of minutes to spare. The rest of the kids are already there, and a hush settles over the room when I walk in. They all look surprised to see me. I nod at a couple of them and hide my smile. Wait till they see how much better I do today.

Peter comes out of the office a minute later, slows as he sees me, then keeps walking to the front of the class. "Okay, folks, gather in a circle."

I drop my bag and hang on the perimeter.

"Before we begin today, I want your input on something," says Peter. "I know it's summer sessions, but I wonder how you'd feel about a showcase on the last day of class."

The kids murmur excitedly. Brittney claps her hands in excitement, grabs Jesse's arm and starts whispering about props and costumes.

I'm still trying to figure out what a showcase is. Mom loves game shows, and a couple of them have something called a showcase. Somehow I don't think Peter's talking about an elaborate setup where we get to guess the prices of cars and groceries, then keep them if we're right.

Peter overhears Brittney's whispering and tosses a smile her way. "It won't be a big or complex production, but I thought it might be fun. I'm covering a mat leave at Vanguard High in September. They've got a great auditorium and dance space. I talked to the principal, and she's fine with us using it for the last day."

This is sounding like Peter wants us to do a performance.

"We'll invite your friends and family."

Yep, definitely a performance.

"What do you think?"

Everyone's nodding. I'm doing the math and the scheduling in my head. I figure there's probably a couple more steps to the choreography Peter was showing us on Tuesday.

If I'm right, then we'll spend a couple of weeks learning that, a couple of weeks learning part two, a couple of weeks for part three and a couple of weeks putting it together and polishing.

When he looks my way, eyebrows raised in question, I drop my hands and give him a quick nod. I'm sure I can do this.

"Great. I'm glad we're all on board. Okay, folks, take your positions." Peter claps his hands, and we fall into four rows.

I'm in the middle of the last row. Jesse's on the end, at the left. I brace myself for his attitude and walk over.

His gaze cuts to me, then flicks away. Ignoring me, he shakes his hands loose and does some small kicks to ready himself for warm-up.

"Uh, hey, listen, you mind if we swap spots?"

His eyes narrow.

I take a breath and opt for the hard truth. "I was a total disaster on Tuesday. I figure if I take an end spot, it's one less person I might crash into, right? 'Cause of the wall."

NATASHA DEEN

Jesse takes a step back as he cocks his head to the right. Of all the reasons he thought I'd give for wanting to trade places, my concern for the other dancers obviously didn't make his list. "Yeah, sure."

We switch spots, and I do a couple of head rolls. I may not be physically ready for class, but my brain's engaged. I remember most of the warm-up and across-the-floor stuff, and I'm determined to show up today.

"Let's start with some gentle head movements," says Peter as he cues the music, then sets down the remote.

*Yeah, buddy, let's start this.*

From head rolls, we move on to stretching our hands to the sky. I'm trying so hard not to grin in triumph. They're baby-easy moves, but I don't care. I'm keeping up, and a glance in the mirror confirms I actually look like I'm part of the class.

In the back of my mind, I'm readying for the demi-plié and grand plié, and I get a wickedly unpleasant shock when Peter says, "Great, let's do some tendus from first position to second, back to first, to the side, back, then back."

I squint past the other dancers, staring through their legs to see what Peter's doing. And it looks like some kind of gentle leg-kick, toe-point thing. Which is easy to say, hard to do.

I try to copy what I see, but while everyone else looks like they're doing a dance move, I look like I'm trying to kick at an invisible soccer ball. And the ball's winning. Winning big-time. I have no balance, so I'm wobbling on my left foot, and when Peter tells us to switch feet, I'm wobbling on my right.

"Luc, turn out your feet!"

What does that even mean? I'm frantically looking at the other kids' feet, trying to figure out Peter's instruction. They're all doing the gentle-kick thing. Is that turning out feet? Maybe I'm swinging, not kicking? I exaggerate the lifting of my foot and get a sharp, "This isn't football, Luc! No kicking. Tendu!"

I go back to watching feet, but looking at other people means one sure thing—I lose sight of my feet and my balance, trip myself and land on the floor.

Peter keeps going.

The kids ignore me.

From that amazing start, Peter moves into something he calls isolations and I call an exercise in futility.

It starts when he tells us to keep our hips in place and shift our chests left, then right. For my efforts, I get a bunch of "Luc, keep the hips immobile" and "Engage your core!" The only bright light is that the other kids are getting stuff like "Straighten your posture!" and "Elongate your spine!"

I'm pathetically happy when he calls time for a break.

The other kids break into little groups. I sit by myself and watch as they help each other practice certain steps. Some I know, most I don't. It makes me wish I hadn't been such an A1 jerk sauce to Brittney and Jesse when classes first began, 'cause right now I could use the help.

Peter calls us back for across the floor, and things only get worse. "Chaîné jeté, chaîné back attitude jump—everyone channel their inner Baryshnikov—and end it with four barrel jumps."

Common sense reminds me there's probably more than one way to warm up and do across the floor, but I was stoked about practicing last class's stuff, and now I'm back to being the guy who knows nothing.

Peter takes his position, then walks and talks us through the chain of movement. "Chaîné in plié on counts one, two. Really resist into the floor."

Resist *into* the floor? What the heck does that even mean?

"Jeté on count three, making sure your hips are square to the direction you're going, and arms are in a V. Turn out of the jump on four. Chaîné in plié again on five, six, and do a back attitude jump this time on count seven, land on eight. Left arm sweeping into a ballet fourth position."

Seriously, I want to curl into a ball somewhere or maybe pour sugar in Coach's gas tank. I can't believe he's making me do this.

"Make sure to press your shoulders down, and lengthen the attitude line of your back leg. Step through with your back leg, and then give me four—yes, four—barrel jumps in a row."

There's a groan from the class.

I suppress my moan.

"Two counts each. Get your hips up, and don't arch your back—you want to be horizontal to the floor! Push into the floor to get up." Peter looks my way. "Luc, you're with me. Let's start off."

I stick my arms out. The first part I can do. It's simple, crossing one leg behind the other, then crossing the leg in front of the other, followed by a low turn and a gentle side leap. The back attitude jump—man, that almost kills me.

Peter's all cool and flexible. He can touch the back of his head with his toes on the jump.

"Cool!" I hear Brittney say. "He added a layout to it!"

Peter's impressing everyone with his skill. I, on the other hand, manage a stuttering baby back arch before my spine and muscles freak out and bring me back—sharply, rudely—to reality. My grunted "Ack!" when the pain hits doesn't help either.

I stumble through the barrel rolls. There's no height, grace or control in my movement. Once again, I'm certain what I've done can't be classified as dance. It might hit the standard for crimes against eyesight though. I ignore the muffled laughter, pretend I haven't pulled another seventeen muscles and watch with a poker face as the other kids take their turns.

In the deepest part of my brain, a little voice starts to whisper that Mom and Dad are right. There are other football teams; there are responsibilities at home. The little voice tells me to quit, and I can't help but wonder if it isn't right. I suck at this, I'm not getting any better—and the moves are getting harder. Why not quit?

# Seven

've never been so glad to see the end of a class in my life. That includes the time Mrs. Hillaby made the guys in English class memorize and recite one of the love sonnets from *Romeo and Juliet*. I regret every stupid assumption I made about dance. It's so much harder than I thought. If I'm going to last through the next two months, I have to seriously up my game. Truth is, I'm not even sure I will last through the summer. That whispering voice has gotten louder and more convincing.

Which means I *definitely* shouldn't be listening to it. It's only been two classes. Plus, I have four days to practice all the stuff. I can't quit. Not this quickly. Not this soon.

I leave the studio and head to the bus stop. While I wait for the bus, I chug my drink and look up *tendu* on my phone. After reviewing a couple of videos, I get what *turn your feet out* means. Instead of having my toes pointing in front, I need my right toes to point right, left toes to point left. Got it. I tuck my phone back in my pocket and make a mental note to ask Peter for a list of the warm-ups and across-the-floor moves he's going to get us to do.

Since I was too stupid to make friends at the studio, I'll have to make Google my new buddy and search out video clips on anything Peter gives me. The bus arrives, and I get to my first job of the day, for the Allisters.

They prefer me to use their push mower over anything gas-powered. I take it from their shed and start cutting the grass. Then it occurs to me that if I'm walking and pushing, maybe I could be doing other stuff too. I can't exactly tendu and cut grass, but I can practice turning out my feet. Using the handles of the mower for balance, I twist my right foot to the right...and get a painful reminder of how *not* flexible I am. I can barely get my toes at a forty-five-degree angle. It takes a couple of tries, but eventually I get a rhythm going.

Turn out foot.

Push lawn mower.

Turn out other foot.

Push lawn mower.

I'm not graceful, fast or worth looking at, but at least I'm practicing. Pas de bourrée as I head to grab a garbage bag, sauté back to where the lawn mower is sitting. I empty the clippings into the bag, then focus on a straight posture and pulled-in abs as I drop the bag at the end of the driveway.

I keep going, using every moment to practice something Peter's taught me. It adds time to my jobs, but since the buses I take to the day's jobs are all on schedule, it's not enough to get me in trouble with Dad. And by the time I'm finishing off my last job, I still can't turn out my feet at a 90-degree angle, but I've got a little more rotation than the 45 I started out with. Okay, so maybe all I can do is a 47 or 50-degree angle, but it's progress. I'm happy to take it.

I do a little pirouette and find the home owner standing in his front doorway with a duffel bag in his hand.

"Hoo, boy." He takes the toothpick from his mouth and heads down the path to me. "I was in the middle of a conference call in my kitchen when I saw you leaping and twirling in the back-yard. I had to end the call."

"Oh, uh, hey, Mr. Hughes." I blush and stammer, "I'm taking dance to make myself a better football player."

He nods. "I heard Lynn Swan did the same thing." He shrugs. "Not sure if it's true or not, but that guy ended up in the Football Hall of Fame, so it can't hurt, can it?"

"No, sir."

"Practice, son, it'll make for perfect." He nods at me, climbs into his Cadillac and drives off.

That's easy for him to say. He's not the one tripping over his feet and making an idiot of himself in class. The part of me that wants to quit has gone from whispering to talking out loud, but I tell it to shut up. Give it a couple more classes, I tell myself. If I don't get better by the end of the month, then I'll quit and take the lecture from Coach.

\* \* \*

Saturday morning comes, and I'm thrilled for a couple of reasons. No lawn mowing, and I'm meeting up with a bunch of guys from the team at the park. We're set to hang, maybe play a game or two. I spend the morning practicing my dance stuff and googling every term I can remember from Peter's classes.

I try not to read the comments in the dance videos. The people doing the instruction look good to me. For sure they look a thousand times better than I do. It ticks me off that they are putting themselves out there and getting criticized for it. I think they're really brave.

In the afternoon I meet up with the football guys and a bunch of other kids from school at the fountain in the middle of the park.

"What?" says Hasselman as he spots me. "No leaping and twirling at the sight of your buddies?"

"Ha-ha." I step into the group. "Funny as a dead frog on the highway."

"I know what the problem is." He points at my jogging pants and shirt. "You're not dressed for it." From behind his back he pulls out a sequined pink tutu.

Everyone laughs. They laugh even harder when Tim puts the rhinestone tiara on my head.

"Wow," I say as I take off the crown. "Did it take all your collective brainpower to come up with that one?"

"Are you kidding?" Tim jerks his thumb in Hasselman's direction. "Thought he was going to have a stroke trying to come up with a good prank."

"I wondered why he was drooling." I set the tiara on Hasselman's blond hair. "Are we going to play or stand around and figure out how to get Hasselman in the tutu?"

We head to an empty field, and everyone takes their spots. I crouch low and realize I've got a little more flexibility in my stance. Hasselman calls the play, and Tim hikes the ball.

I explode backward, pursue to the right and spin off an attempted block by Tim. There's a quick second, a spark in my brain, when I notice there's no twinge in my knee. Two dance classes, and I'm already seeing results.

I speed right to cut Hasselman off.

He drops farther back, looking for his receiver, but I'm on him so fast there's no time for him to even throw the ball. I throw him to the turf. "Not on my watch." There are no warning pings in my joints. Usually when I pull that move, I'm hoping I don't hurt myself.

"Ugh." Hasselman rolls over. "Is it me, or are you faster than usual?"

"You noticed it too, huh?" I stretch out my hand, grab his and haul him up.

"Nice twirl on the tackle," says Hasselman. "Those classes may not make you a better football player, but they sure make you a prettier one to look at. Try and memorize some good steps. Maybe we can do up a cool end-zone dance."

Tim snaps his fingers. "Yeah, and definitely a team one for when we win next year's championship."

I can barely dance, and these lug nuts want me to choreograph them.

I smile.

It's nice to be part of a team.

# Eight

Tuesday morning comes. I've spent the last four days practicing, practicing, practicing. I don't know how I look when I'm doing all the stretches and steps, but I know how I feel. Flexible. Today I was able to touch my toes and put my palms flat on the floor. I've never been able to do that before. Plus, all the practice is making me aware of muscle groups and connections I don't normally use. If I keep going like this, the effect on my football is going to be phenomenal.

But if I'm going to be 100 percent committed to dance, it means fixing the mistakes I've made. And that starts with figuring out a way to undo the stupid first impression I made with the kids. What I'd really like is to start from scratch. That's impossible, so before class I head to the coffee shop for a takeout order of coffee for fifteen, plus donuts for the sugar fiends and bran muffins for the health freaks. I don't think it'll win me any friends or forgiveness, but if it gets some of them glaring at me a little less, I'll take it. It's hard enough to keep up. I don't need the mirrored view of their disapproval too.

The traffic elves must be in a good mood today, because it's all green lights and clear roads to the studio. I get in early. Brittney, Jesse and Peter are the only ones in the room when I arrive.

"Hey." I hold up the food in my hands. "Uh, I thought I'd bring a mid-morning snack." I wait as they do a once-over of the bag and cardboard thermos of coffee.

They glance at each other, then back at me.

Peter gives me a small half smile and takes a step back.

One down. Two to go.

"The coffee will be cold by then," says Jesse, "but I'll take some stuff now."

"Yeah." I smile. "For sure."

Peter clears a space on the table for me to set everything down. Brittney and Jesse help unload the creamers and sugar.

"That was nice of you," says Brittney.

I'd say thanks, but her tone suggests complete surprise that I'm capable of human decency. So I nod and say, "Yeah, no prob."

A few minutes later the rest of the kids trickle in. Peter gives everyone a few minutes to grab a quick coffee and makes sure the class knows I'm the one who brought it. I get a few grudging nods. I'm happy to take them.

"Okay, guys." Peter claps his hands. "Take your last sips, and let's get into formation."

I swallow the last of my coffee and take my spot at the back. My heart's hammering. Four days of practice. I know I feel the difference, but will Peter see it?

"Let's start nice and easy." He drops his head to his chest, then slowly raises it again.

I follow along.

"Great. Now add in the shoulders, relax to the floor, let your hands hang loose and free..."

I know no one else is paying attention to me. No one else can feel the contraction and stretch in my hamstrings and quads as Peter instructs us to touch our toes, then bend our knees and press our palms to the floor. The tug of my muscles is a victory. The feel of the dust on the palm of my hand is as welcome as the cold metal of a trophy.

We move through the half hour. My favorite move is when he gets us to lie on our backs, lift one leg into the air, cross it over our body and bring it back to the floor. A quick glance shows Brittney and Jesse doing their Jell-O-for-bones impression. My leg is bent, not straight, as I bring it into the air, and instead of keeping my back on the floor, my entire body twists with the rotation. Peter's yelling, "Core, Luc!", but I don't care. All I know is, with practice I'm going to get better. And in getting better, I'm going to dominate the football field.

By the time we move to across the floor, I'm sweating, my quads are trembling, and my knees are pinging.

"We're going to do something a little different today," says Peter. "Instead of across the floor, I'd like us to do some improv."

My legs are trembling for a whole new reason now. Improv? Like, get up and do a dance?

Peter claps his hands. "Spread out. This time let's see what movements you can do from one side of the room to the other, using big leg movements as your stimulus. Think kicks, battements or swings."

Peter's doing a count. I don't know why. Am I supposed to do the isolation in time?

I do a magnificent impression of a tree trunk and watch the other kids.

Brittney's doing a wicked standing leg split, and Jesse's ninja stance is awesome. A kid in the front row does a kick into a flip.

"No showboating," Peter tells her. "Actual isolation." He turns his focus to me and tilts his head as if waiting to see what I can do.

Which is nothing.

The only thing in my brain is the crane kick from the old-school version of the Karate Kid movie I watched with Mom and Dad. I roll the dice and do it.

Peter dips his head, and I'm pretty sure he's trying not to laugh.

"You're wobbling," he says. "Do some relevés. Five, six, seven, eight, on your toes—up, down, up, down. Hold on your toes." Peter comes over. "Higher—extend yourself. Balls of your feet, Luc, get on the balls of your feet! Good! Lengthen your body. Imagine you're a puppet. There's a string going through the top of your head, and someone's pulling you up straight. Tighten your core—"

*Imagine I'm a puppet and someone's pulling my strings?* I'm Pinocchio to his Geppetto. My big toe is hurting from the weight, but I keep at it, even though I'm listing back and forth like a sail caught in the wind.

"That's better," he says after my tenth attempt. "But your balance is terrible. You need to work on it." He turns and heads to another student. "And your posture," he tosses over his shoulder. "Work on how you stand."

I sigh and drop my heels to the floor. I've been standing since I was eight months old. Hard to believe I still don't know how to do it correctly.

Peter calls a break, and I grab my water. As I drink, I lift my heels, then drop them. Lift. Drop. I keep an eye on myself in the mirror, thinking about strings in my head and inner cores.

"Bring it back, folks. Instead of choreo today, I want us to explore the Martha Graham style of dance—"

"What?" The question is out of my mouth before I can stop it. "But what about the showcase and practicing for that?" The kids are staring. Blood is creeping to the outermost layers of my skin.

"How about if we do the run-through after some Martha time?" Peter suggests.

"Uh, yeah, sure. Sorry, I didn't mean to interrupt."

"No problem," he says. "I'm glad you're practicing and taking this seriously." Peter's gaze scans the class. "In Martha Graham's style of dance, the torso is central to movement. Your relationship to the dance is based on gravity, time and space. She experimented with the dynamic between contraction and release."

The kids are nodding, and I'm lost.

Peter sits on the floor and spreads his legs into a split. "She loved sharp movements." He stretches his arms to the ceiling and flips his head back. Then he pushes his upper body to the floor like he's trying to give the ground a head butt, stops short and jerks himself back to an upright position.

I don't know who Martha Graham is, but I'm impressed with that kind of muscle control.

His eyes are bright as he talks about her influence on the culture of dance, her focus on everyday experience as the subject of dance and how her political views influenced her choreography. "She turned down Hitler's invitation to perform at the International Arts Festival that was to run at the same time as the Berlin Olympics," he says. "Instead she choreographed *Chronicle*, which spoke out against fascism."

Wow. Turning down Hitler? That was brave, but then to make up an entire dance in protest of his style of government? I'm googling this woman when I get home.

Peter rises to his feet. "She wasn't about representing emotion as much as she was about *becoming* the emotion. That's what I want us to work on today."

We move to the wall while he steps into the middle of the dance floor. He cues the music, and an instrumental song plays.

I'm watching, memorizing, thinking I can get into Martha Graham. Her movements are sharp, deliberate. Hand to the sky, jerk down, back to the sky. Backward torso spin. Then something that looks like karate-chopping the air, flowing into some kind of windmill arm-torso spin.

Peter has us repeat the movements across the floor.

I'm surprised when Jesse takes a spot opposite me.

He doesn't acknowledge that it's me and not Brittney, so I don't know if he deliberately teamed with me or if he wasn't paying attention. But I've got Martha Graham on my mind.

When it's our turn, I do my best to imitate what I've seen.

"Luc! You're dancing," says Peter. "You're not a Klingon trying to overthrow some invisible enemy!"

What does that even mean? The next time, I try to scale back on the emotion and get some comment about zombie dancing.

It doesn't get any better when Peter takes us through the choreography. As the opening chords of Jussie Smollett's "Conqueror" start to play, I take my spot. My heart is doing a rev-stutter. All I remember from the routine is to lift my hands one at a time, go on tiptoes—one at a time but in sync with my hands—then drop my hands to my face. That's only the first move and five seconds of the routine. What am I supposed to do with the other four minutes?

Peter's hard on everyone, telling Brittney she has to control her turns, Jesse to put more power into his leaps, and me...I can't seem to do anything right.

"Maybe it's too hard," says Peter. "Maybe we should do something simpler."

I know what he's doing, because Coach does the same thing. It's a reverse-psychology move. He tells us the play's too difficult. Then we try harder because we don't want to be the guys who couldn't do it.

The studio kids are no different.

"We can do it."

"Give us some time."

Time. I thought I'd used mine wisely in practicing, but today's session seems to prove I just can't do it. This is the third class. There should have been some improvement, but if Peter's comments are true, I'm not gaining any ground. The voice is back in my head, telling me to give up. Or try another studio. And this time, it's more than a whisper.

"I'll think about it," says Peter. "We'll see how you guys do next class, then go from there." He ends the session. I head to my bag.

"Hey."

I turn to face Brittney.

"You were good out there today."

"No, I wasn't."

She laughs. "Okay, but you were better, a *lot* better. Keep practicing."

"Don't let Peter get in your head," says Jesse as he comes up. "He's like Oscar the Grouch. Grumpy and usually talking trash." He glances over his shoulder at the clock. "Come on, B, that smoothie won't wait."

They turn to go, but I stop them. "Uh, listen, I want to say sorry about that first day. I was late and in a bad mood...I acted like a jerk, and I'm sorry."

They nod. "Thanks for the coffee," says Brittney.

I grab my bag and head for the exit.

"Luc, wait."

Oh man. I turn, wary, to face Peter. "Yeah?"

"What's your cell number?"

I give it to him.

"Okay." He's concentrating on his screen, his fingers tapping on the keyboard.

A few seconds later, there are four bings on my phone.

"These are some videos that might help you," he says. "They break down some of the more complex movements we've been practicing."

"Oh, wow, okay." I open my phone and check the links. "Uh, thanks." I meet his gaze. "But today, I thought I sucked."

"You did." He claps me on the back. "But you sucked forward. I respect that. See you next class." He pivots and walks to his office.

Huh. A smile tugs at my lips as I head to work. And the voice in my head is quiet.

# Nine

"We talked about Martha Graham last class," Peter says after our warm-up in Thursday's class. "Today I want to talk to you about Katherine Dunham."

A couple of kids in front of me whisper excitedly to each other, but the name means nothing to me.

I've spent the last two days watching the videos Peter gave me, then doing my best to mimic what I see. Today I'm going to suck it up and buy a big mirror to lean against the wall in the basement. I'm not thrilled with the thought of watching myself mess up, but I have no one to spot for me, so I'll have to use the mirror to gauge my posture and movement.

"Katherine Dunham invigorated modern dance," Peter says.

The videos Peter had sent me talked about the history of contemporary dance, how it was born from ballet and set out to embrace a less rigid style and allow the dancer more freedom of movement. That's as much as I'd gotten before I moved the tracker to the spots where I saw dancing. I respected Peter's wanting me to understand the history of contemporary dance, but I wasn't looking to do this professionally. I only wanted to learn enough to help my football career and quiet down Coach.

"She was born in Chicago in 1909 and didn't start dancing until her late teens." Peter looks directly at me as he says this.

I'm trying to catch the hint. Is he telling me that if a woman who didn't start dancing until she was almost an adult could do it well enough to have influenced the entire genre, I need to work harder? Or is he trying to help me stay positive? Like, *Hey, man, she didn't start until she was older, and look how far she got. There's hope for you.*

"After she graduated with a degree in anthropology—" Peter's gaze is back on me.

An anthropologist who became a dancer? How is that relevant to me?

"—she traveled to the West Indies to study anthropology and dance, and that's when her life shifted. She came back and infused modern dance with Caribbean influences—limb isolations, flexing of the torso—"

Once again I'm completely lost. I lean into Jesse and whisper, "Why's he talking about modern dance in the middle of a contemporary class?"

"Contemporary dance is influenced by a huge range of dance styles," Jesse whispers back. "That's what makes it so incredible."

"Oh." I tune back into Peter's lecture.

"Dunham used her troupe and her stage to protest segregation and civil rights. Shows such as *Southland* brought the issue of lynching to the stage—"

My brain whirls to imagine what this would look like. I'm definitely searching that out online tonight.

"—and her work for racial equality has been credited with inspiring the Brazilian law that forbids racial discrimination in public places."

I'm doing the math on all of this and feeling—once again—like dance is handing my butt to me. The fact that I know nothing about dance history makes me feel like a Class A dunce. Up until now, I've figured dance was all tutus and twirls, leaps and spandex. But it's more than my small-minded definition. I'm going to go back over those videos Peter sent, and this time I'll sit through the narration and voice-overs.

"Today I want us to play with her style of dance." He cues the music, and a reggae-calypso song pushes through the speakers.

He brings one knee to his chest. Then the other knee to his chest. Both feet down, large chest roll, then some kind of jumping-jack thing—except it's right hand up, bring it to the left foot as the left foot comes up, then do it with the other hand-foot combination...and then I'm lost on the steps. But I'm loving the music and the energy.

"What is this? Katherine Durham?" I ask Brittney.

"Dunham. It's Afro-Haitian dance."

"It's very cool." I lean in and whisper, "What's he doing? Can you give me the steps?"

A quick frown wrinkles her forehead. "I can give you some, but contemporary is different than something like ballet or tap. Some movements in contemporary don't really have terms. It's about the action." Her head's bopping to the music. "Okay, we've got isolation, isolation, wide second position, spotting, contract, release, undulations. This isn't in order, you know. He's moving too fast."

It's awesome, like judo put to music. When Peter finishes and before he can get us into across-the-floor formation, I ask him to do it again.

He shrugs and gets into position.

I grab my phone and hit *Record* as he moves through the choreography.

When it's our turn, I'm first in line, along with Jesse. I'm going to get it wrong and look like an idiot anyway, so I may as well go first and get it over with.

Peter walks us through it.

I bring my arms up and out, parallel to the floor. In time with the music, I bend my elbows and bring my hands to my chest, then push them out again. I glance in the mirror. Spaghetti arms. I do it again, but this time I pretend the air is twenty pounds as I push my hands back parallel to the floor.

The contraction and release of my biceps and forearms give weight to the movement, and the reflection in the mirror looks a hundred times better than before. I push my chest out, bring it back in like a vertical chest wave. Then I do it again as I pretend I'm high-stepping on hot coals.

The names I give the movements would probably make the studio kids laugh, but I don't care. It helps me to keep up with Peter and to get the steps right.

We get to the knee-to-chest move. I pretend there's weight pushing me up and down, and the movement looks sharper, tighter. Arms back up, push out my chest, roll it back in like a snake wave. That must be the undulation Brittney mentioned. I push the thought aside and hurry to keep time with the music and the movements. There are a couple of quick-step movements— kicking my heels out and then to the side—that leave me breathless, but I love the footwork. I can imagine using it to get around a difficult offensive guard. Same thing with the kick and turn. That could work when I have to deke around a player.

I go through the rest of the steps and get to the other side.

Peter nods for Jesse and me to clear the space, then motions for the next pair of kids to start.

"That was decent," says Jesse. He grabs for his water bottle and hands me mine.

"Thanks." I can barely get the word out. The choreography Peter had us doing was big movements, quick kicks and side steps. I'm as winded as when I run the track.

"You're getting better," he says. "It seems like you're really getting into it."

I gulp my water and nod. "I get together with my football buddies and play. You know, keep in shape for fall. You wouldn't believe how much better I am."

"I believe it."

"But I'm not where I want to be."

Jesse shrugs. "It's practice."

I shake my head. "No, it's more than that."

"Not really. If you can walk, stand, hop and kick, you can dance. You just have to get it into your muscle memory."

"Well, I think my muscle memory is Swiss cheese."

He takes a long sip of his water. "You want some help?"

I straighten. "You'll give me some tips?"

"I can do that, but I can also practice with you."

There's a moment of shocked silence. Jesse actually helping me is more than I'd hoped for. "Uh, yeah," I stammer. Then I grin. "Man, that would be awesome."

He nods, satisfied. "Me and Brittney will whip you into shape."

"That's great. Thanks."

Jesse gives me a grin. "You suck like a high-end vacuum, but you try so hard. I hate to admit it, on account of what a jerk you were to us at the beginning, but you're inspiring." He punches me on the shoulder. "In, like, a car wreck kind of way, so don't get all egotistical about it or anything."

"I'm the most humble car wreck of a vacuum you'll ever see."

He laughs, and we go back to watching the across-the-floor exercises.

* * *

I get home after work and sit down to dinner. Mom and Dad are halfway through their pot roast and mashed potatoes. Dad hands me the platter of grilled asparagus. "Things are looking up," he says. "You made it home before dessert."

"I told you I'd make this work."

"We had a few new clients sign up today." Dad lifts his fork of gravy-laden mashed potatoes, watching me carefully. "That means adding another house or two to your route." There's a deliberate pause, and then Dad asks, "Is that going to be a problem?"

"Nope. I'll get it done."

"You know the bylaws forbid us from working after ten at night."

I roll my eyes. "I haven't been that late."

"Just giving you a heads-up."

I stack my plate with food and lay into the asparagus. "By the way—and thanks for asking— the dance class is going well."

"Of course it's going well," says Mom. "You're an amazing athlete."

"And dancer, according to Dan Hughes." Dad glances at Mom and hits me with a sly smile. "Something about seeing your pirouette when you were packing the clippings."

Heat rises in my cheeks.

"Are you practicing while working, or are you just that happy to have a summer job?"

I keep my head down and stuff a mouthful of meat and veggies into my mouth. "Didn't think there'd be a problem with multitasking."

"Son, you can whistle, shimmy or mambo while you work as long as you work and get the job done." He pauses. "On time. If practicing is delaying you—"

"It's not!"

"Then we're fine."

"Luc, I'll need the car all next week," says Mom.

I know it's immature to be annoyed that I'm losing the car for a day, but it feels like a giant inconvenience. "Uh, sure, but how is that going to work for Tuesday? Tim and I team up on Wednesdays, but—"

"Come to work with me," says Dad. "I've got a big job and need your help anyway."

"I can't miss class."

"One class isn't going to kill you."

I snort. Considering how fast the classes go and how hard I'm struggling to keep up, missing class might not kill me, but it could definitely give me serious injury. "No, Dad, I can't skip a class. Coach is expecting—"

"I don't care what your coach is expecting, Luc." Dad puts down his fork, steeples his fingers and gives me a death glare. "This family is your number-one priority."

"I thought getting an education was my number-one priority."

"Don't be a smart aleck. Your education *is* a priority—"

"And a football scholarship is pretty big on the list."

"Yes," Dad concedes. "But it's not on the top of the list. Will a scholarship help the family with your university tuition? Sure, but why do you have to play for Marshall to get it?"

"Because Coach is the best in the city."

"There are a lot of great coaches in town. If this one can't understand you missing one silly class—"

My ears turn hot at the word *silly*.

"—then he's not the coach for you. Miss the Tuesday class and come to work with me. We'll do your route and mine."

I'm barely keeping up at dance, and now I'm missing a class. I eat the rest of my dinner even though it tastes like cardboard.

\* \* \*

The next morning I email the studio to tell Peter I won't be at the class. Then I climb into the truck and head with Dad to our first job. It's at a factory that produces frozen food. The bosses must like their employees, because there's a ton of lawn space, with picnic tables, trees and flower gardens.

"They have a John Deere in the shed," says Dad as he hands me the key. "Go ahead and start while I get started on the gardens."

I don't answer him as I take the key and walk to the shed. The nice thing about the mower is that I don't have to bag anything. The downside is that I'll be sitting for the next two hours.

I start it up, hop on and head to the part of the grounds farthest from my dad. I wonder what the class will be doing today and worry that Peter may have changed the choreography. The noise of the mower is too loud for me to use my earbuds and listen to the music from the showcase, but I hum the tune in my head and walk through the steps in my imagination.

Of course, in my imagination I'm a lot more coordinated and graceful than in real life. I figure it's because I don't have the movements fully memorized. Practice, I remind myself. I'll get there.

It takes every bit of the two hours to mow the lawn, and in the meantime the sun has gotten higher and hotter. The unending chug of the mower's engine comes to a blissful stop as I bring the vehicle in and park it in the shed. For a moment, I sit. It's musty in here. Between the dust, the lack of insulation and the heat, the place smells like a combination of oil and hay and dirt. But it's shady, and even if it's just a few degrees cooler in here than outside, I'm happy to take it.

"You contemplating life or the futility of cutting grass only to have it grow again?"

I swing off the lawn mower and ignore Dad's question. "Are you done?" I ask.

"Yeah."

My shoulder brushes his as I push past. "Then let's get to the next job," I say. "Time's money, right?"

He doesn't say anything. He doesn't have to. The thin line of his mouth speaks his anger, but I don't care. I'm mad too. I head across the grass, barely acknowledging how good the wind feels on my skin. I get to the car, climb in and slam the door.

"You slam that door again and you lose all access to the family vehicles." Dad climbs inside and shuts his door. "You can be as mad as you want to be, but that doesn't give you the right to disrespect property. Especially property you don't own. Are we clear?"

I give him a sharp nod of my head and stop myself from saluting.

Dad exhales an angry breath. "You know, I was going to see if you wanted a shake before our next job, but if this is your attitude, then forget it."

"I'm not thirsty anyway." Not true. I would've loved a milkshake.

The rest of the day is like this. Us barely talking. When the final bag of clippings is dropped at the end of the driveway of the last client, we climb back into the truck. I wait for Dad to start the vehicle.

The day's been a scorcher, and even with the windows down, the interior is furnace hot.

"Dad, are we going to go?"

He's still sitting, staring out the front windshield.

"Do you need me to drive?"

"No," he says, "I need you to grow up."

His words sting.

"Do you have any idea how selfish you've been this summer?"

"That's not fair!"

"Neither are you." He scowls. "Your mom and I have been really good about giving you time to pursue this dance thing, and look how you've shown your gratitude. You're late *getting* to work for me and late *finishing* work. You're missing out on family activities. Worst of all, I found out this morning that you're nagging your mom for the car on Thursdays."

"I asked one time!"

"You shouldn't have asked at all! Your mom shares *her* car with you. And all she asks is that you step off for one day. You can't give her that?"

"You don't understand!"

Dad shakes his head, disgusted. "The fact you're even arguing with me says how selfish you're being."

My mouth snaps shut, and I cross my arms, fuming.

"You're always talking about team effort, but you can't seem to get it through your head that this family is a team." Dad starts the truck. "Frankly, if this were a sports team, I'd have cut you a long time ago for your bad attitude." He puts the vehicle in gear and pulls onto the road.

And, of course, we hit some kind of traffic jam or accident, so we're totally stuck in the hot silence together. In my mind, the argument continues. *I may be selfish,* I tell him, *but at least I help out in the house. What about you? It's not like you've got an extra set of work that eats up three hours of your day. And it's not like you're working for two bosses. But I am. You and Coach. And how am I supposed to get by when the two of you give me instructions that conflict with each other?*

*Miss class,* says Dad.

*I better not hear about you missing class,* says Coach.

I slouch down in the seat and stare at the cars idling beside us. My big plan to out-silence my dad crumbles under the weight of my righteous indignation. "You're not being fair," I tell him.

"It's not like you're trying to juggle work and sports and family."

Dad's laugh surprises me. "Boy, kid, you are full of something. You think what? I work, then come home and sit around watching TV?"

"Well—"

"You think the groceries buy themselves and the cars get tuned up by themselves and we have a laundry fairy that—"

"Okay, okay. Geez."

"Your mom and I may not play sports when the day's done, but we have responsibilities too." He turns to me, and he's got that look on his face like he's annoyed with me but also loves me. "When's the last time you went to the fridge and there wasn't milk?"

I shrug.

"And last week when you asked me to come outside and throw the ball around with you, what did I do?"

My indignation is a lot less righteous as it morphs into embarrassment. "You helped me."

"Right away, or was I doing stuff?"

"You were doing stuff, but you said in fifteen minutes—"

"And?"

"And you were in the backyard in fifteen minutes."

"You may not understand or even agree with me and your mom when we tell you to take out the garbage right away. And you may not like it when I tell you that clients' lawns have to be done by a certain time. But it's not up to you to understand or agree." He pauses for breath. "It's up to you to respect it."

Man, if I get any smaller, I'm going to drown in my clothes.

"All summer I've watched you go the extra mile for your coach and your dance instructor, and I can't figure out why you don't do the same thing for your mom and me."

"I'm sorry," I mumble. I clear my throat and try again, louder. "I'm sorry."

"I appreciate it, son, but I don't need you to be sorry. I need you to do your part to make this summer work, okay?"

I nod. "Okay."

The silence is back, but it's a warm silence.

"Your mom said you wanted the car tonight. Something about running an errand?"

"Uh, yeah." Given our conversation, I'll feel kind of stupid telling him what it is.

"What do you need to do?"

"Oh. I wanted a mirror for downstairs, so I could watch myself when I practice." I wait for a long sigh or another conversation about my being over-focused on myself.

Instead, Dad says, "You want to do it now? Get it over and done with so you don't have to go back out again?"

He's offering, but I can tell by his tone that he's not thrilled about my reason for needing the car. Still, he's trying to be nice, and I don't want to be a jerk. "Yeah, sure. Uh, maybe I can buy you a shake as thanks?"

Dad smiles. "You know what you need to do to show me you're grateful, but I'll take the shake. A double shake."

"There's no such thing."

"I'll invent it."

I laugh and roll my eyes.

The traffic inches forward. "I want to listen to the sports news for a bit," he says. "Why don't you text your friends and see what you missed today?"

The tone's still there, but I'm willing to do what he says. Partly 'cause I need to know what I missed, but partly so we have a reason to stop talking. "Okay."

I text Jesse. When he responds, I'm not happy to read that Peter has changed around the choreography.

**How much?**

**We should meet up. Brittney and I can catch you up.**

**Is it hard?**

**Only if you don't practice.**

I read his text, then read it again. That's code for *yes*. I'm sure of it. Man. I've just had it out with Dad about not letting him and Mom down with chores and work, and now Jesse's telling me I'll have to practice even harder. Where am I going to find the time?

# Ten

After dinner I head to Jesse's house. I park on the street, then head up the sidewalk and ring the bell. A few seconds later I see his figure through the beveled-glass inset in the door.

"Hey," he says, letting me in. "Brittney's downstairs. We have the house to ourselves, so feel free to shout in pain and frustration when you see what Peter's added."

Oh man.

He closes the door and walks across the tile into the kitchen. "Help me bring down the water, okay?"

"No problem." I grab a set of glasses as he takes the pitcher. We head down a spiral staircase into a walkout basement. At the bottom of the steps, on the left, is a family room with couches and a TV. It's the space on the right, though, that has my attention.

Hardwood floors, a barre that runs the length of one wall, mirrors on two sides, windows on the third.

"Whoa. You take your dancing seriously."

Brittney rises from where she's sitting in the middle of the space. "I know, right? I've tried to convince my dads to do the same thing, but they're all about the pool table."

"Perks of being an only kid," says Jesse. "And having a mom who used to dance professionally. It's really her space. Well, ours now."

"No wonder you're so good," I say.

"Are you crediting my genetics over my work ethic?" Jesse asks.

"What? No!"

He laughs and slaps me on the back. "I'm messing with you."

Whew. "So how hard is the new choreography?"

"Worry about that later," says Brittney. "We think part of your problem is that you're so caught up in the routine, you're forgetting about having fun with the movement. Let's just move, have some fun and play around. We'll do some warm-up, maybe isolations, and across the floor." She gives me a cheeky smile. "And maybe some improv so we can see that awesome crane kick again."

"Ha-ha."

We stand in a line.

"Inhale and lift your arms up," Brittney says, taking the lead. "Exhale down. And again."

From there, she moves us through shoulder rotations, then chest circles and into undulations.

"I wish you did warm-up," I tell her as she gets us to shift our hips left and then right. "I can actually keep up with you." From the corner of my eye, I take a quick glance at my reflection. "And I don't look like a total dope doing it."

She laughs. "This isn't the warm-up. This is just for you, to get your muscles a little loose so we can really warm up."

My anxiety shows in my reflection in the mirror.

Jesse cackles. "Maybe I should have brought some heating pads too."

That's the last thing we get to say before Brittney takes us through a warm-up that would leave Peter crying for mercy. Her ballet training shows—she has us doing advanced work. Développé. Frappé. And all this time, I thought frappé was a kind of drink.

"Let's use the barre," she says, and waves us over.

I've never done work with a barre. "Am I going to have to put my heels on this? 'Cause I saw it in a movie once, and I'm telling you, I'm not that bendable."

"It'll be fine," she assures me. "Keep a little distance between you and the barre. Now bring your heels into your body, do a small plié up and lift your right foot so your toes are above your left knee."

Even after weeks of practice, first position still hurts my knees.

Brittney catches the flicker of discomfort that crosses my face. Frowning, she looks down at my feet. "You need to follow the natural turn-out of your feet, or else you'll stress your knees." She drops into a sitting position and stares at my feet with the intensity of a foot doctor about to diagnose a fungus. "Turn out for me. It should come from pulling up in the thighs and rotating them back." She gives me an encouraging smile. "That part is pretty integral."

I bring my heels together and swivel my toes out.

"There! Stop! That's your natural position."

"But my feet don't look as turned out as yours or Jesse's."

"Don't compare," she says. "You have to do what's comfortable for your body or you'll risk injury."

Point taken.

"Hmm, can you center your weight on your toes? Don't roll into the inside or outside."

I close my eyes, shift my weight to my toes and feel the difference in the way my pelvis shifts. My body seems to lengthen.

"Okay. Good." She rises and stands beside me. "Let's try it again. Hold the barre for balance, plié up, lift your foot..."

I spring on my toes, lift the other foot and hold the position.

"Great! Now let go of the barre and balance."

Oh boy. My grip releases from the barre, one finger at a time, then hovers a few inches off the wood. I last a split second before my body starts wobbling.

"Come on, Luc! Get those stabilizing muscles to kick in!"

"Easy for you to say!" I grab for the barre and shoot her an envious look. It's like her toes are glued to the floor.

Jesse's not as balanced as she is, but he's more balanced than I am.

"Let me try again." This time I don't try for the move like she says. Instead, I go on tiptoe with my right foot, then slowly lift my left foot so the toes are above my knee. Once I'm sure I'm in position, I let go. I crunch my abs, push my shoulders back. And wobble a little less.

From there Brittney takes us through a bunch of stretches and positions that involve the barre. Most of the terms go over my head, but I get—and appreciate—what she's doing. She's getting me to stretch to increase my flexibility and balance.

After a half hour we take a quick break to grab some water, and then it's Jesse's turn. "For across-the-floor work," he says, "I'm going to mix up a bunch of styles."

"Okay." I stand by the wall and watch.

"Start with your left foot, then step. Look at what I'm doing. Step forward and swing your leg in a half circle, dragging the toes a little on the floor. Then do the same with the next foot and make sure you finish with your foot directly in front of your body."

"Kind of like the walk models do on the runway," says Britney, "but keep your hips silent."

I follow along and pretend there's a steel rod in my spine so my torso stays straight.

"Right hand to the sky, bend forward, sweep your hand across the floor..."

My fingers trail against the floor. I feel a surge of pride as I realize my hands can do more than sweep. They can drag against the wood. A few weeks ago, I could barely touch my toes. I grin at my progress, then tune back in to Jesse.

"Come back to standing, bring the right hand across the body and touch your left hip."

"What's this move called?" I ask.

Jesse stops and drops his hands. "No, no terminology today. I think that might be part of your problem."

"One of your many, many problems," Brittney adds, giggling.

"You're so focused on the vocabulary," says Jesse, "that you're forgetting there's a movement behind it. Maybe if we get you moving without talking steps, choreo or routine it might free you up to dance."

It's a fair argument. "Like in football, instead of saying we'll do a stutter-step drill, it's pound your feet, then move where Coach points the ball."

"Exactly."

"Okay. It's not like it'll hurt my progress." I point my finger at Brittney and give her a fake glare. "No comments."

She raises her hands and shakes her head.

"Let's try it."

We start again. Strut, hand to heaven, back to hip, spin down into something like a reverse-warrior pose, into a wide second position. I stop dancing.

So do Brittney and Jesse.

"What's wrong?" asks Brittney.

"It's in my head," I say. "I can't help but name the steps in my head."

"I get you," says Jesse. "It's like when I was learning French. I'd think of the English sentence, translate it to French and then reverse it when the other person answered. I had to get to the point where I was thinking in French and listening in French."

"Maybe we're going about this all wrong," says Brittney.

"What do you mean?" I ask.

"Well, teaching you to dance. Maybe what we should do is just put on the music and let you dance."

That stops my heart. "But I can't dance."

She rolls her eyes. "Fine. Maybe we should put on some music and let you move to music."

"Uh..."

Jesse snaps his fingers. "You have warm-up for football, right?"

"Yeah."

"What about football drills to music?" Jesse suggests. "You do those all the time, right?"

"You mean, like, strike and shed, or reroute and react?"

He blinks, then laughs. "Okay, I understand your pain when we throw down dance terms. I've got no idea what you're talking about."

"Show us," says Brittney.

"Here?"

Jesse nods. "Yeah."

"I need a tackling sled and a tackling dummy for one, and a ball for the other."

"I would forgive you for calling me a dummy and step in," says Brittney, "but the *tackling* part is putting me off."

"Just pretend." Jesse waves at me like I'm a stubborn baby bird refusing to fly. "Go ahead and show us."

I shrug and nod. First up, the strike and shed. I get into ready stance, pretend I hear the whistle and explode forward. Run. Hard stop. Pretend I hit the sled, then run laterally left, another hard stop, then speed forward and go for the invisible dummy.

Without stopping for a breath, I run back to the center of the room and get into position again.

"Wait, wait! That's perfect—let's do that move," Jesse says.

I stand still. "Okay."

Jesse heads over to the dock. "I want you to do what you just did but in slow motion."

"What?"

"Slow motion."

"Because...?"

"Uh-uh! Remember the deal! No questions, and no more crane kicks."

"I'm never living down the Karate Kid, am I?" I groan.

"Not while either one of us or our descendants is alive," Jesse says with a cackle. "C'mon, bro. Do what you gotta do. Except slow."

He turns on the music, and it's super slow.

"Are you kidding me?"

"It's Sade, 'No Ordinary Love.' It'll help you remember to go slow."

"It'll put me to sleep."

"Stop wasting time. Football slow."

"Yeah, yeah."

It's crazy hard to run in slow motion, but it's even harder to ignore the music. I keep time with the slow beats, run, lift my hand to the imaginary tackle. Sidestep, sidestep, again and again, then run forward.

"Okay, good." Brittney shuts off the music. "Now this time when you run, drag your feet like someone's holding your ankles."

I do it again, even though it hurts to have the top of my foot slide across the floor.

"Nice," says Jesse. "Now, when you do your imaginary push, you're pushing from your chest out."

"Right."

"Okay, push from the chest up, then hold your hands for a beat or two, reach skyward, then bring it back down..."

"Oh!" I catch what they're trying to do. "How about a spin before the lateral runs? Then, instead of high steps for the lateral, I can do—" I cross my right foot over my left, then drag my left foot, kick my right foot behind and drag my left foot again.

"Nice! Go for it!"

The Sade music starts again, and I slow my movement, slow my breath. Enjoy the stretch of my hands reaching up. I go on my toes for the spin, then bend my knees and purposely stumble into the horizontal steps.

Brittney and Jesse clap.

"One final thing," says Brittney.

"Okay, what?"

"I heard that the song is Sade's interpretation of 'The Little Mermaid.' That in the song, the mermaid gives up everything to be with the prince, but in.

the end he doesn't love her back, and she's forever stuck on land, alone."

"Wow, that's depressing."

"I know, right?" Brittney's eyes are bright with excitement.

I laugh. "Psycho. Look how gleeful you are about it!"

She punches my arm. "Focus. What I'm saying is that it's a great song to play around with emotionally speaking. So do that dance again, but this time pretend you're the main character in the song. You've given up everything for someone who'll never love you back."

I don't have to pretend. That's basically what happened to me and my ex-girlfriend. Six months later, it still stings to think of her.

"I'm going to let the song play all the way through," says Jesse. "Keep going. Either repeat what you did or start modifying other football drills."

I nod. "Uh, I'm a little nervous."

"We'll all do it," says Brittney. "Improv, right?"

We each take a corner of the floor, and Jesse cues the music. I go through the strike and shed a couple of times, but as the song progresses and she's singing that she gave all her love and he took it, I'm back in time, hearing my ex tell me she doesn't love me anymore.

Usually when those feelings come, I push them down, pretend they don't exist. This time I take a deep breath, because I know it's going to hurt, and let the emotions run through me. When I extend my hands, those emotions make my fingers tremble. They give weight to my roll, they're the gravity that pulls me back when I leap, and they give flexibility to the arch in my back.

When the song is done, I'm sweating, and I feel hollow inside. It's not a bad empty—more like there's nothing inside because I left it all on the floor. I wipe the sweat from my face and look up to see Jesse and Brittney watching me. "What?" The question comes out like a croak.

"That was amazing," says Brittney. "You were raw, and the moves weren't polished at all, but the emotion—"

"It was there, and it was awesome," Jesse says. "You know, when you let go, you've got talent."

"Thanks, but I don't think Peter's going to let me run football drills and call it contemporary."

"Yeah, but you know, you're always worried about being good enough," Jesse says, his expression thoughtful. "I think you proved you are good enough."

"With you, it's all about the practice," Brittney says. "You did amazing with the drill-dance because it's in your muscle memory. You just have to rehearse the choreo until it's embedded in your muscles."

Jesse shakes his head. "He's got the choreo. What he doesn't have is the confidence."

They exchange long looks. Then they look at me.

Uh-oh.

# Eleven

"I can't believe you convinced me to do this," I grumble as we walk through the metal gates of the park entrance.

"You know it's for your own good," says Jesse.

"No, I think this is material for you to laugh at me."

Jesse stops walking and looks at me, his face serious. "I would *never* laugh at you for doing something like this."

"Yeah," Brittney agrees. "Dancing is hard work, and performing in front of people can be terrifying. No one will laugh at you."

Somehow, I doubt it. Maybe I was light-headed after the workout at Jesse's, or maybe it was the giddiness of having done something close to actual dance, but when the guys suggested doing the routine at the park, where everyone can see me, I found myself saying yes. Not at first, of course, but somehow—and I still don't know how—they managed to get me to agree.

We walk along the tree-lined path. The park sits in the center of downtown, and it's full of man-made lakes, fountains, picnic spots and foot bridges. And right now, at noon on Saturday afternoon, it's chock-full of families and groups enjoying the sunshine and warm temperatures.

I do a quick scan to see if any of my football buddies are around. They're still buying me leotards and hair gel so I can *put my hair into a nice tidy bun.* If they're here, for sure I'm going to get heckled and for sure I'll forget my steps.

But they're not as terrifying as all the people milling about. There's a bunch of moms with their babies and toddlers. A few families bicycle past. Couples line the benches, and others walk by us with their hands linked. "Let's do it by the fountain," says Brittney. "The ground is nice and flat."

"I'd rather do the routine on the grass," I say. "It'll make it less painful when I fall on my face." That gets me a shot in the arm.

Jesse adds words to Brittney's punch. "Don't say that."

"But what if I screw up or forget a move?"

"Then do your football-dance thing," says Jesse. "It's contemporary dance—it's fluid and allows for autonomy. Besides, the only people who know the routine are the three of us. Anyone else is going to think you're doing a solo section."

We get to the spot, a grassy area with a big fountain in the middle. Benches border the grass. Off to my left is a group of people doing tai chi, and farther down the grass some junior high kids are playing soccer.

Brittney casts a critical eye around the area. "Luc, you're right."

"Great," I say, not bothering to ask what exactly I'm right about. "Let's go."

"No, I mean about doing the routine on the grass." She points to the right. "Over there looks good." Not bothering to look back, she heads to the spot and starts to stretch.

Jesse follows.

I can't back out, so I trail behind.

"Do you remember the warm-up from yesterday?" he asks.

I nod.

"Okay, let's do that for ten minutes, then the routine." He sets down his portable speakers by a tree while Brittney and I fall in line with each other. Jesse stands between us, cues the music and starts. It's the basic stuff we did last night—head rolls, sweeping our arms up and then down and into a stretch to touch our toes.

The warm-up doesn't take away my nerves, but a few minutes in, when I realize most people aren't watching and don't care, my anxiety level drops from terrified to highly stressed.

At the ten-minute mark, Brittney moves us into the routine.

I gulp some air, take heart from the fact the area is less crowded than before and move into the choreography. The instrumental music for "Conqueror" swells. A soft *boom* of the drum counts me in.

*Five, six, seven, eight*—I step into the routine.

*One, two*—

Rise up on the toes of my left foot, quickly follow with the right. At the same time, I do the marionette wrists, pretend my puppeteer pulls the strings of the right hand, then the left.

The pretending helps. My arms are jerky, sharp. I let my hands fall to my face—and accidentally slap myself.

I ignore the surge of embarrassment at the slipup and remind myself that no one but me knows I messed up. I follow that with a head roll, go into a spin, fall into a side roll. Roll out of it into a slow-motion run. Drop into a crouch, sweep into a standing position, drag my fingers along the ground.

Bend my knees, sweep my left foot out and into a semicircle as I swing it behind my body. Keep myself in a down position, pivot on my right leg.

I realize I'm counting. More than counting. I'm doing it out loud. My lips ticking the beats and the steps. I glance over at Jesse, then Brittney, and confirm what I already know— they're in the zone.

I stop, waving my arm like a helicopter rotor. "Can we start again?"

They stop dancing. "Yeah, sure."

Jesse resets the music.

I take my position. Take a breath. Feel the wind against my face. Inhale the smell of summer and sun. Hear the leaves of the trees rustle. Hear the start of the music. Feel the rhythm inside. Jussie Smollett's voice comes through the speaker, and I pretend I'm him, singing about the endless cycle of life, the victories and defeats. Then I'm in those moments, the first time I saw my ex, the day she said goodbye.

I keep dancing, and when he gets to the part about being a conqueror, I *feel* it. It's in me, the energy of the dance and the music. He's singing about standing strong, about being authentic and true to myself rather than following the crowd.

"I am a conqueror," he sings, and I want to sing along with him.

I am a conqueror. All the injuries I've taken for football, all the cold, rainy mornings when I ran track, playing through the pain of an injury, the feel of an opposing player's arms around my waist as he tackles me, the feel of his waist in my hands as I drag him into the mud and dirt.

The song is my life. It's my theme song. It's me fighting with Mom and Dad to take dance class and stick with football. It's me finally learning the steps. It's all hitting me as the music swells and dips, and even though it's breaking my heart into a million shining, brilliant pieces, it gives me confidence to make eye contact with one of the people who has stopped to watch.

He gives me a trembling smile and a thumbs-up.

I'm dancing, and he's in a wheelchair.

But he stays.

Watches.

Cheers me on with a smile and a gesture.

And that's when I see it.

Feel it.

This song isn't mine—it isn't my life. It's *everyone's* life. All the people watching, this is their story as well as mine. And I keep going, hitting the beats harder, punching my elbow into the air. I don't know this guy, but I find myself dancing for him, making my body move in ways his can't. And it doesn't make any sense. I don't know if he even cares that he can't walk. But I want him to watch me and *feel* like he's walking. I want everyone watching to feel like they can fly when they see me dance.

There's an energy in the air, a current, and it's thrumming through me. I'm sweating from the cardio in the dance, the sun beating down on me, the wring of emotion as it twists me and spirals into the crowd.

But it's not a spiral—it's a boomerang. It rockets around the people watching, spotlighting their reactions. They're connecting with us—with me—because of the dance.

I never thought I could say so much without ever opening my mouth.

By the time the song ends, the audience has grown to a group of fifteen. They applaud as the last chord echoes into silence. Jesse and Brittney smile and bow. Me too, but I feel like I should be applauding them. Thanking them for what they've given me.

For me, football has always been a metaphor for war and battle. I run onto the field and I'm a warrior, ready to defeat my foes and grind them to dust. The people who come to watch either cheer for or against me. Like me, they are looking for victory.

I thought dance would be the same, the audience cheering me on—but it's not. They're not rooting *for* me, they're rooting *with* me. In every bend and kick, hop and step, they were connected to me. It was my body that was moving, but it felt like all of our hearts were beating in sync.

I've never felt a high like this before. If the football field is my favorite spot on earth, then I think I just found my second.

And it's a dance floor.

*   *   *

Saturday's moment in the park triggered an inner avalanche, and I spend the rest of the weekend practicing in every spare moment. Actually, I find myself *making* moments for practice. When I grab the broom to sweep the kitchen, I cross the floor with a set of chaînés, or turns, complete with my elbows up and out like I'm holding a beach ball.

Or when I take out the garbage, I mix pas de bourrée, sauté and jeté. It has Mom laughing and Dad rolling his eyes, but I don't care. The more I know the steps, the more I can let go and embrace the movement. The showcase is coming up, and I want to get the same reaction from that audience as I did from the people at the park. I'm hooked.

I can't wait for Tuesday.

* * *

On Monday, I'm up an hour early so I can get in some practice before heading to my first job. It's for Mrs. Peabody, who lives in a house that looks like it came straight out of the board game Clue. Her backyard is a giant square with trees and circular beds of flowers, and it's perfect for mowing and dancing.

Traffic's light, and when I arrive she's on her porch, having her morning cup of coffee. I wave hello, then unpack the mower and bags and head to the backyard. At stoplights during the drive, I practiced chest, arm and foot isolations, but before I start mowing-dance practice, I take a couple of minutes to stretch out my legs and hips. Then I turn the mower on and start cutting grass while I practice the routine and run through some of the warm-up exercises.

I'm so into the movement, how it stretches and lengthens my hamstrings and calves, that I don't notice the gopher hole...until I step right into it, wrench my ankle and fall. My heart jumps as I grab the mower handle for balance and the entire thing tips back. With visions of the blades slicing and dicing me, my body takes over and does an instinctive twist that saves me from the blades, but my entire left leg takes the force of the fall. There's a *pop* in my knee, an answering *click* in my ankle, and then I'm down on the ground and curling into a ball. The pain is sharp and hot. Have I done the unthinkable? Have I hurt myself so badly I may have ended not only my chance to dance in the showcase, but to play football again?

# Twelve

I t turns out to be just a sprain, but it still messes me up. I have to miss two classes plus work. Even though I can't dance, I still go to practice and watch and video the class. And since I can't mow lawns, I spend my work time in the office, fielding calls and helping the staff with paperwork. In my off time, I watch the video and practice modified versions of the choreography.

When I meet the guys to watch them play football, I spend the first quarter splitting my time between tracking the game and reviewing the video for the showcase. By halftime, 25 percent of my time is going to watching football. The guys are almost at the end of the fourth quarter when I realize I missed the third and don't even know what the score is.

And that's when it *really* hits me.

Sometime during the past few weeks, dance sneaked up and surpassed football as the number-one priority in my life. I watch the final play of the game and try to figure out when it happened, but it's like falling in love. It hits when you're not paying attention.

I want to dance. I think about it all the time. I practice in my head when I'm at work, when I'm at home. I've started searching out videos on my own and learning steps by myself.

This is what I want to do with the rest of my life.

The doubts crowd my mind. I've always been a footballer—and my family has carried the burden of fees, game times and practices. How are they going to react when I tell them I want to change focus and step away from football—and a shot at the NFL? And what about dance? I'm barely keeping up now. How do I think I'm going to keep up with the kids who've been dancing since they were three? Sure, Katherine Dunham didn't start dancing until her late teens, but she's Katherine Dunham. I'm just Luc Waldon.

But even as I'm trying to talk myself out of it, the possibility of being a dancer makes my heart race. I'm excited by the challenge. I want to do this more than anything else I've ever done.

Tim whoops, looks over and gives me a thumbs-up.

Man, the guys. My family. How do I tell them any of this? I take a breath and realize my life has gotten a lot more complicated.

* * *

I spend the last two weeks before the showcase ignoring the questions, the doubts and the fears. As soon as I'm allowed back on my feet, I'm practicing, practicing, practicing with Brittney and Jesse. Heck, I'm even doing the routine in between mowing lawns with Tim.

But no matter how hard I practice, how much lawn mowing I do, I can't fight the small voice asking me what I plan on doing with my life—and how I plan to tell my family. I want to wuss out. Just stay quiet. Tell Mom and Dad that I want to keep up with dance because it improves my game.

They'd buy it. The guys and Coach would buy it.

But it would be a lie. And when I actually start getting traction on the dancing, then what?

How will I explain needing more time to practice or take classes?

In the end, it's Katherine Dunham and Martha Graham that save me.

They kick my butt.

It's the day before the showcase. I drop Tim off at home and head back to my place. I'm running through the routine in my head, running through the past two months, and I think about the classes that focused on the dance styles of Dunham and Graham.

And what I remember is Peter telling us that Katherine didn't start dancing until she was around my age...and that both women used their talents to take on discrimination, dictators, racism and genocide.

It makes me ashamed.

If those two women stood up for what they believed—and did it in a time when women weren't considered equal and minorities *for sure* weren't considered equal—then what am I doing lying about my goals? And what does it say about me if I'm deceitful going into a dance style that's all about having integrity?

Of course, *saying* I'm going to be brave is a

lot easier than actually *being* brave. So I compromise. I text Tim and the guys, tell them to bring their tiaras and tutus to Vanguard School 'cause I'll be performing. And at dinner that night, I tell Mom and Dad about the showcase and say they're welcome to come.

"You paid for it. Well, 90 percent of it," I say. "Maybe you want to see what your money bought."

They glance at each other and agree to come.

Part of me is glad. I want everyone to see me dance so they'll understand the decision I'm making. But part of me is terrified. What if I do a terrible job? If I bomb, how will I ever convince them to let me pursue dance as a profession?

\* \* \*

I'm backstage, watching from behind the curtains as the audience trickles in. No surprise, the football team takes the first row. I keep watching. Mom and Dad show up, see the guys, wave and take seats a few rows back.

"How are you doing?" asks Jesse.

I told him and Brittney about my plan to focus

on dance as a profession when I arrived at the school. "Okay. Trying not to throw up."

He laughs. "It'll be fine," he says. "But if you *do* start puking during the routine, aim for any part of the stage that doesn't have me on it."

Peter arrives and waves me over. "You did a really good job this summer," he says. "I know you only took this class because you needed it for football, but if you ever want to continue, I want you to know I'd be happy to be your instructor."

I'm too overwhelmed to do anything but stammer a thanks. Before I can say anything more, he slaps me on the shoulder and goes onstage. He welcomes everyone and talks a bit about the class. Then he introduces us and walks off.

We come out and take our spots. My heart is smashing against my ribs, pounding so hard I think it's going to explode, and my lungs can't seem to take in enough air. I'm too scared to look at my family or my friends.

"Go, Luc!" Tim yells and starts clapping.

A few of the guys on the team follow his lead.

There's nothing but honest support in the cheer, and it gives me the courage to look up and make eye contact. Everyone, Mom and Dad included, have open, sincere expressions on their faces. And it reminds me of being in the park, about the people watching. And I remind myself that this performance isn't about me. It's not about proving anything. It's about giving to the people watching. About making them feel glad they gave up their time to sit in the plastic chairs. About reminding them of the bad and good things in life.

The music starts. All the practice, all the running through the routine in my head, and I'm golden. I *know* this choreography. I know where everyone on the stage will be, how and where they'll move. I have control over my space. I have autonomy. And I have muscle memory.

My body sinks into the first step. Hands up, left and then right, tiptoes in sync. Drop my hands to my face. I remember all the times I let myself down or life disappointed me. I run my hands along my forehead and cheeks, channeling that pain and transmitting it to the audience in the shameful drop of my head.

I keep the emotion charged and running through my body. When it's time to do the leg extensions, I'm pushing hard, elongating my limbs as much as I can, feeling the stretch in my tendons as my stabilizing muscles kick in. I remember Peter's dance on the first day of class when it's time to reach my hands to the audience. I imagine my arms and fingers growing, lengthening, touching the audience.

I make eye contact with Tim. Try to tell him through my movements about all the times I've seen him fail and all the times I've been so proud to be his friend because he got back up and tried again. The combination of emotion and physical exertion is more than I've experienced before, because I'm tapped into the audience, feeding off their energy and feeding them back mine.

Sweat's pouring off my body, my breath's coming in pants, my muscles strain to keep my balance and control, but I push through. I have something to say about standing and fighting, about staying true to yourself. I'm not giving up until I transmit all my words and thoughts and feelings through my dance.

The final note of the song fades into silence, and I rest on the last move, a power stance—feet shoulders' width apart, arms strong and by my side, the courageous expression of a warrior on my face. There's a brief silence, and then the crowd is applauding. Tim and the guys are the loudest of all.

# Thirteen

"You were amazing!" Mom gives me a giant hug, then shrieks at how wet and stinky I am.

Dad hugs me too. "You look like you sweated off five pounds up there." He grips my shoulder and squeezes. "You worked really hard up there. I'm proud of you."

"I did good, huh?"

"You looked like a pro," says Mom.

I take a breath and rush in before fear can stop me. "I've been thinking..." My voice fails for a second. "I want to drop track, swimming and soccer and focus on dance and football." My mouth is suddenly dry, but I push on. "I want to dance for a living. I know I'm starting late and it'll take a lot of work. But I'm good at football, and I figure I've got a good shot at a scholarship. I can do a Fine Arts degree with a focus on dance. I know it's really physical, and I'll really have to give it some hard thought if I'm drafted or something—"

Dad breaks in. "Listen, Mean Joe Green, why don't we dial back on what you'll do if the NFL comes calling and live in the moment for a second?"

I brace myself for a lecture—or, worse, a no.

"I think it's a good plan."

I gape at him. "You do?"

"Honey," says Mom, "it's obvious how much you love this. Everyone could see it in the way you danced. And you really did look like a pro. If that's what you were able to do in two months, I know you'll do great."

"Scaling back on your other sports is a smart idea," says Dad. "And it shows you're thinking about school and work and what your priorities are." He smiles. "If this is what you want, your mom and I will support it. I don't think it's easy to make it as a professional dancer, but maybe if you had an education degree or a physical-therapy degree to go along with it..."

I don't know what to say. It's gone way better and smoother than I'd hoped. And I'm saved from any babbling when Tim and Hasselman come up.

"Nice job." Tim smacks me on the back. "You made Hasselman cry."

"That was dust in the auditorium," Hasselman shoots back.

"Yeah." Tim makes quotes with his fingers. "Dust."

"Hey, listen." Hasselman shuffles, then shoots a furtive look at Mom and Dad, who take the hint and move off. "Do you know if those classes are running in the fall?"

"The dance classes?"

He nods.

"Yeah, why?"

Tim and Hasselman glance at each other. "No one can argue how much better you're playing 'cause of it," says Tim. "We're thinking about signing up. After all, if Coach thinks it's worthwhile..."

"Yeah, sure. Come on. I'll introduce you to Peter."

I take them over and make introductions, and they start talking. Then I see Jess and Brittney coming toward us.

"Hey," I say, stepping away from Tim, Hasselman and Peter.

"We saw you talking to your folks," says Jesse. "How did it go?"

I smile. "I'm going to be a dancer."

# Acknowledgments

Many thanks to Marla Albiston, Lucas Crockett, Jessie Dugan and Brittney Schmidt for all their help with my contemporary dance research, editor extraordinaire Robin Stevenson for her keen eye and supportive spirit, and the gang at Orca for all their behind-the-scenes work on this book.